FALSE SIGHT

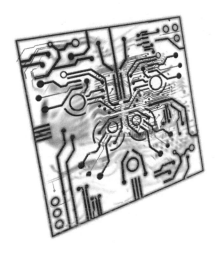

FALSE SIGHT

DAN KROKOS

Hyperion

New York

First Edition

3 5 7 9 10 8 6 4 2 1

G475-5664-5-13152

Printed in the United States of America

This text is set in 12-point Cochin.

Library of Congress Cataloging-in-Publication Data
Krokos, Dan.
   False sight/Dan Krokos.—First edition.
      pages cm
   Sequel to: False memory.
   Summary: "After discovering the truth about her origins—she is a clone, created to be a weapon—Miranda must fight to protect those she loves from an unthinkable future"—Provided by publisher.
   ISBN-13: 978-1-4231-4985-9
   ISBN-10: 1-4231-4985-8
   [1. Cloning—Fiction.   2. Genetic engineering—Fiction.
3. Science fiction.]   I. Title.
   PZ7.K9185Fc 2013
   [Fic]—dc23   2013010342

Reinforced binding

Visit www.un-requiredreading.com

SUSTAINABLE FORESTRY INITIATIVE Certified Sourcing
www.sfiprogram.org
SFI-00993

THIS LABEL APPLIES TO TEXT STOCK

to Jack Smith,
the bravest man I've ever known

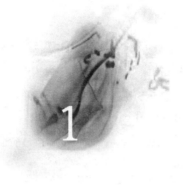

Thomas David asks me about my eyes.

Over and over again.

"Are they seriously red? Let me see and I'll stop asking. Kristin, let me see."

Kristin isn't my real name. It's Miranda. Kristin is pretty generic, but that's the point. And at least I don't have two first names, like Thomas David, the boy who keeps asking about my eyes.

"They're not bloodshot," Thomas says to me. "Gina says the irises are red like a vampire's. Hey." He pokes my arm. His fingernail is a little too long, so it bites into me.

Keep it together. Do not react.

"Don't react," I say aloud by accident.

"What?" Thomas leans over his desk so he can see my face better. "Say again?"

If he were a Rose, making him stop wouldn't be an issue. But Thomas David is not like me; he's fragile. We can't sort it out with fists. Not that a normal girl would use fists. I don't know what a normal girl would do.

"Kristin, if you have red eyes, that's okay. It's kind of hot. I love vampires."

The teacher is rambling about the global economy and how the markets interact. She hasn't looked back in five minutes. Noah is slumped on the other side of the room, dozing. Doom impends for the entire world, yet economics can bore him into relaxation. Then his face turns toward me a millimeter, and his eyelashes flutter. The boredom is an act; he's watching us.

"Gina said you're crazy. She said you hit her. Are you going to hit me? Hey, Kristin."

Gina Daly first saw my eyes in the girls' bathroom. She caught me cleaning my contacts. I wear them to cover my red irises, because red eyes freak people out. The colored contacts turn them a muddy brown color no one looks at twice.

Gina didn't notice them at first. She started with, "How'd you get that scar?" Her nose wrinkled like she smelled something bad. The horizontal slash on my cheek is just a thin white line now, but it's still obvious. Rumors have already spread about it—that my dad gave it to me as a kid, that I did it to myself, that I let a boy do it. They say I have more scars hidden by my clothing, probably self-inflicted. To me, it's just a mark on my face that reminds me I don't belong here. I am not a normal student with normal problems, no matter how badly I want to be.

So when Gina asked about the scar and how I got it, I told her, "A sword," because it's true. I kept my eyes down and scrubbed the contact in my palm.

"Whoa, let me see your eyes." She put her hand on my shoulder and tried to *turn* me.

I've killed people and had people try to kill me. So when Gina Daly, just a regular girl with regular problems, moved me against my will, it got to me. She was not dangerous or scary—I know, because I am familiar with those things.

I put my hand on her throat and shoved her away, maybe too hard. She stumbled until her back slammed against the hair dryer.

"What is your *problem*?" she spat.

"You touched me."

She looked directly into my eyes. My right one was muddy brown, and my left, bright red. My eyes are blood-colored because they're colored with blood. I'll get to that later.

Her anger melted into disgust. "What is *up* with your eye?"

I turned back to the mirror, pulled my lower lid down,

and popped the lens into place. "Nothing. What's wrong with your face?"

Gina curled her lip. "Okay, Snake Eyes."

She clacked out of the bathroom in her heels, and I became Snake Eyes. Snakes don't even have red eyes. I looked in the mirror at my scar. At my lank auburn hair and the bluish veins around my eyes. I thought about makeup and nail polish and other things girls use. I didn't know where to start, and a part of me was confused about why I didn't care to.

My new name spread through school in a day, and people started asking to see my eyes sans contacts. They asked Sequel, my "twin," what the story was. She was slightly more abrasive with her responses, especially when someone noticed she wore contacts too.

Peter stopped me outside my locker a few days later. He kissed me lightly, took my books, and leaned against the dark green lockers. "We need to talk."

I shut my locker and spun the dial. "What's up?" I knew what was up.

"You punched a girl and she told the entire school about your eyes."

I started walking to economics, wondering again why we were pretending to be real students. "I didn't punch her. I shoved. And I acknowledge it was a stupid thing to do."

"It wasn't stupid. You reacted, that's all. If you had thought about it first, then it'd be stupid." He smiled, almost.

I nodded, unsure of what to say.

He grabbed my arm and gently pulled me to a stop. People streamed past us on both sides. A rogue book bag hit me in the kidneys, but I didn't budge. "It wasn't your fault, *but* . . . Noah and Rhys think we need to move on. People are starting to talk." His blue eyes dropped to my scar. "With your scar, and now your eyes . . ."

"Yeah?"

His eyes went right back to mine, which I was grateful for. "I'm just saying we should think about it. You're not attached to this place, are you?"

I wasn't, but I didn't like the idea that we *had* to move. This was our grand attempt to put the past behind us. Moving somewhere else wouldn't fix the problem.

Peter leaned in to kiss my forehead. When he pulled away, he was smiling, which made me smile on reflex. "Just think about it. We can start over a hundred times."

I wanted to ask him to just make a decision, but in the last few months our roles have become less defined. Peter was always our leader, but without something actively trying to kill us, it's been hard to tell who's in charge, if anyone.

"You're smart," I said. "And cute."

"I know. Just think about it," he said, squeezing my hand. Then he entered the stream of moving bodies and disappeared.

Now I'm in economics and Thomas David won't stop asking about my eyes.

"If you don't answer me," Thomas says, "I'm seriously gonna touch your eye."

Keep it together. Do not react.

I need Noah to do something. If Thomas sees Noah perk up, he'll stop, because Noah is scary. He can put this dead look on his face that needs no words. The best I can do is glare, which only seems to egg Thomas on. I'd have to make a scene to shut him up, and I already discovered that's a bad idea. My frustration is manifesting as prickly neck sweat.

I shear the eraser off my pencil and roll it between my fingers.

"Why are you being weird about it?" Thomas David says.

I toss the eraser at Noah. It hits him in the ear. His lip twitches, but the rest of him stays still. Maybe he wants to see if I can handle the situation in a nonviolent manner, which I can't blame him for. If I had shoved Gina just a little harder, she might've ended up in a wheelchair.

"He can't save you," Thomas says, after making sure Noah didn't notice.

I finally look at Thomas's face. He's sneering, the way

people do when they're trying hard to show they're amused or having fun. His lips are like pale worms, glistening with spit.

"Hi," he says. "Now just move your contact. A quick peek."

He reaches out like he's going to touch my eye.

I don't know if he actually would have; he never gets that far. I reach out too, grab his index finger, and bend the whole thing back a few degrees. I stop before it breaks, because I'm in control. It probably still hurts.

For some reason, Thomas David opens his mouth and screams. Everyone jumps in their seats.

"She broke my finger!"

"I did not," I say calmly.

The teacher turns around and lowers her glasses. On the blackboard behind her it says CHINA VS INDIA VS US???

"He tried to touch me," I say, as if that will explain everything. Thomas David is clutching his finger, so nobody can see it's not really broken.

Noah rolls his eyes at me. Thomas David gets sent to the nurse, and I get sent to the principal.

I sit in a stiff chair until Principal Wilch calls me into his office. He tells me to sit in another stiff chair across from his desk.

"What's the problem?" he says.

I tell him a version of the truth. I say I have a rare corneal disease that discolors my irises and Thomas David would just not stop making fun of me and he even tried to touch my eye, and I just—I snapped, and I'm so sorry, I didn't mean to grab his finger.

"What should I do about this?" Wilch asks. He folds his hands over his substantial belly and leans back in his chair. "I can't have students assaulting each other. Even if Thomas David is a punk."

I don't point out that the finger in question is, in fact, unbroken.

"Give me a warning?" *Get me out of here.*

"Will it happen again?"

"Not unless he tries to touch my eye...." Wilch's brow furrows. Wrong answer. "I mean, no. It won't happen again."

"That's good. I want you in this office on your off-periods. We need aides."

I have a strange feeling I won't be around to comply. So I just nod and say thanks and leave his office.

Noah is waiting for me in the hallway. "You're lucky they didn't call the cops," he says.

I pick at my jeans. "Why? His finger's fine."

"What was the guy saying?"

It sounds kind of silly now.

"He wanted to see my eyes. He wouldn't shut up about it." A girl carrying a hall pass walks by and gives me a funny look. I ignore it. *Don't react.*

Noah doesn't say anything. I can't tell if he's not amused or just pretending to be not amused.

"He was going to touch my eye."

"Uh-huh. Well, Rhys wants to meet us in the gym."

"Did you tell him what happened?" I think I know what the meeting will be about, if he did.

"I texted that you were going to the principal's office."

"Thanks for telling on me."

"Hey. I told him you didn't do anything wrong."

We start walking toward the gym. My shoes pinch my feet, and my jeans and shirt make me feel naked. Give me my armor any day.

"Just relax," Noah says. His hand briefly massages the knots in my neck. Thomas David is probably already telling everyone what a psycho I am. Noah takes his hand away before I have to tell him to remove it.

In the gym, Peter and Rhys are playing one-on-one under the hoop while Sequel stands off to the side, disinterested. Rhys jumps three feet off the ground and sinks a jump shot over Peter's head. Peter gets the rebound and stops dribbling when he sees us.

"What's wrong?" I ask, hoping I don't sound defensive from the start.

"Nothing," Peter says. "I just thought it was time for a chat."

"We're leaving," Rhys says.

Peter sighs. "Thank you, Rhys."

"But don't feel bad," Rhys adds quickly. "If you hadn't pushed that girl, one of us would've gotten in trouble eventually."

"That probably doesn't make her feel better," Sequel says. We're biologically identical, but Sequel's hair is dyed black and styled in a pixie cut. Changing her hair was one of the first things she did—we had found her in the lab with shoulder-length auburn hair, exactly like mine.

Noah says, "Look, we knew we'd stick out here. So we learn from the experience. We don't make the same mistakes at the next school." He's making eye contact with Sequel while he says it, even though he's talking to all of us. It's cute he thinks we don't notice the way they look at each other. Cute in a lead-ball-in-my-stomach kind of way. I swallow and pretend I don't care, mainly because I don't know *why* I care. I should be glad —if Noah and Sequel really do have some kind of romance going on, then I don't have to worry about what he thinks of me and Peter being together.

Rhys holds his hands up and Peter passes the ball. Rhys sinks another jump shot. "Screw going to another school. I don't see the point. We're smarter than these imbeciles. I should be *teaching* calculus." The ball rolls back to his feet, and he picks it up and shoots again, nothing but net. "What good is school when the creators plan to conquer the world?"

He's got a point. Once we figure out what the creators are up to—creators, as in the people who cloned themselves to create us, and who gave us the ability to create mass panic with only the power of our minds—we'll have to stop pretending to be real people and start trying to save the world. Or something along those lines.

Going to school is just a distraction until that time comes. It started with the question *How do a bunch of kids raised as super-soldiers live normal lives?* The answer is they don't. But the decision to try came one night after a brutal training session on the roof of our apartment building. We'd been talking about it for the last hour. Bruised and achy, we pulled ourselves into a loose huddle that was almost like a group hug. It was corny, but we did it every time after training. We just stood like that as our breathing returned to normal. It reminded us that we were the only family we had, and that we couldn't afford to let things come between us. Not anything. And so far we'd done a pretty good job of that.

"The creators will show up again," Peter said. "Count on it. But until then, we should try to live. Otherwise what are we doing?"

Rhys smiled. "I could take a dose of real life."

I was in. I wanted homework, and a locker. I wanted to try it all. One day we might need social security numbers and diplomas. After that was the possibility of real jobs, with paychecks and health benefits. I could work in an office, have my own desk with pictures of people I love on it. I could go home to a family and think about what to do for dinner instead of how to avoid becoming a slave.

What good is school when the creators plan to conquer the world? Rhys says now.

Peter gets the rebound again and tucks the ball against his hip. "You have a point," he says to Rhys. "Noah?"

Noah bites his lower lip and looks at each of us in turn. "I don't know. Is school really hurting us in the meantime? I mean until we have to fight again."

If school makes us softer in the long run, then yes, it's hurting us. We should train more. There's a reason none of us have been able to relax here. The creators haunt every shadow. They are every stranger on the street. They're our unfinished business. And living each day with eyes in the back of your head is no life at all.

In unison, our watches begin to beep. Time for our memory shots. Without speaking, we each pull syringes from our bags. My thumb pushes the lemonade-colored liquid into my arm, and a fist unclenches in my stomach; for a little while longer, my memories are safe. I imagine how this looks to someone else—five kids sticking needles in their arms under a basketball hoop.

"Can we just decide tomorrow?" Sequel says, capping and pocketing her syringe. "After homecoming. I already bought my dress. Let's do normal one more day, okay? Then we can go to Prague for all I care."

Rhys tosses the ball up, but it bangs off the front of the rim. "Fine, we stay another day." He's only agreeing because he already picked out nice clothes for the dance. The girls like him, and he likes that they like him.

"Fine," Peter says.

I don't care what we can do, we're still teenagers. While I'm not sure hanging around is the best idea, it isn't selfish to grasp at a few extra days of normalcy.

Not selfish—just an error.

I had my run-in with Thomas David just a little too late. Because staying that extra day turns out to be the biggest mistake we've ever made.

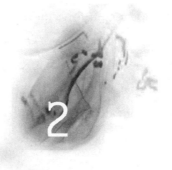

2

A few months ago I was inside a plastic cylinder, suspended in some kind of nutrient-rich, blue-green gel. My childhood consists of fragments of memories left over from the girl before me, the Miranda North I replaced. Those false memories now swim in my head with the real ones I've created since my body was pulled out of a tank.

The girl who lived before me was part of a team, and now I'm part of that team. The closest description of us would be *supersoldiers*. We're the deadliest people on earth. We can create fear in others just by using our minds. Our brains burn so hot, we have to take medicine to keep our memories intact.

The people who created us, who we're cloned from, have

bad plans for us. We're still trying to figure out what those plans are.

We trashed our creators' lab and melted the whole thing down. The creators had hoped to make more of us—clone after clone—with the same skills and knowledge. I'm proof of that.

We found a memory inside a machine the creators built to store our personalities. The memory was put there by my creator, Mrs. North. Through Mrs. North's eyes, I saw her meeting with the Original Miranda—oh, yeah, turns out my creator is just a clone too. In the memory, Mrs. North asked to see the Original's new secret weapon. All she knew was that the weapons were monsters—monsters with a name she was afraid to say or even think. Monsters to be used in some kind of worldwide attack, working alongside us. *The ones who will conquer the world,* Mrs. North had said in place of a name. Hard to get clearer than that, while still giving us exactly no idea of what we're up against.

For now, feeling normal isn't realistic, but sometimes, for a second or two, I forget I'm not really a person. I try not to let it happen too often, because when reality crashes back, it's in the form of a lead chain around my neck.

I dance with Peter in the gym for most of the evening, through the fast and slow songs.

My fingers are clasped behind his neck, and his hands are on my hips. His eyes are too blue to be real. Like blue glass lit from within. I miss his hair. It used to be long enough to curl at his neck, but now it's short and bristly, as black as his eyes are blue.

We don't talk much, which is nice. Peter doesn't have to fill any voids. There are no awkward silences with him. We just dance, and I breathe him in and feel his pulse on my cheek when I lay my head alongside his neck. In this moment I feel normal.

We're in a sea of our slow-spinning classmates. Every few revolutions I see Rhys dancing with some girl I don't recognize. He smiles at me with a vertical worry line between his eyebrows. His dancing partner doesn't know he murdered his teammates in the forest one calm summer day. I doubt she'd dance so close if she did.

I'm wondering where Noah and Sequel are when Noah appears on my right. He barges between me and Peter, shattering the calm.

"Cutting in!" Noah says with this big awkward smile. He slips into Peter's place so fast, my hands are still in the air. "Place this hand here," Noah says, putting one on his shoulder. "And this one here." He holds my other hand in his and keeps a good amount of space between us, unlike all the other dancers.

I can't tell if I'm more angry or embarrassed. Peter doesn't

16

mention my past with Noah, ever, and whenever these situations come up, I'm the one who's painfully aware. I catch Peter's eyes but he rolls them, dismissing the situation. He knows Noah isn't a threat.

"What if I don't want to dance with you?" I say. My palms are sweaty and they shouldn't be. I have no reason to be nervous. But suddenly I can't meet his eyes.

"Nonsense, all the ladies want to dance with me." To Peter, he says, "Chaste enough?" They smell the same, like the one bottle of sample cologne I saw on the bathroom counter at home.

I'm still frozen, refusing to dance. Peter might pretend he's fine with it, but he has to be a little upset. Just a little.

"Chaste enough," Peter says. "Watch your hands." I catch him staring at the back of Noah's head for a half second. Anger under his skin; he does care.

"All right then," Noah says to Peter. "Sequel is lonely now. Go help." He spins me away, and Peter melds into the crowd.

"Hey, beautiful," he says to me with a happy grin. I'm always startled to see a smile on *any* of us. Nothing weighs Noah down. I find myself smiling back before I can stop.

"Hey, obnoxious," I say. I shouldn't be doing this. I should pull away.

The smile droops into a mock sad face. "Aww, am I? Surprised Pete didn't try to crush my head."

"He knows you're not a threat," I say. "And maybe your little secret isn't so secret. You ever think of that?"

His eyebrows shoot up. "Of what secret do you speak?"

I just stare at him.

He blinks slowly, defeated. "All right, you got me. Yes, I like her. Is that weird? Of course it's weird." Now *he* won't meet my eyes.

The song ends. I give his hand a squeeze. "It's okay, Noah. I want you to be happy." I put as much sincerity as I can in my voice. Because it should be okay. No reason for it not to be. Sure, it's hard looking at him without remembering the kiss under the water, which saved my life. And the first night he told me he loved me. My past with him is a mixture of real and false memories, and sometimes it's hard to tell them apart.

All I have to do is remember I'm not that girl and it becomes easier. I'm not the girl he loved. He doesn't know that, though. I'd tell him so it could be easy for him too, but the circumstances of the first Miranda's death would destroy him. Noah stole her memories to keep her safe, because he loved her. And all it did was get her killed.

Even now I feel what the girl before me felt, all alone in that alley. Rain pounded down, soaking her. Something punched her chest—it felt exactly like that, a punch. She fell on rough wet concrete. Then the blood was pumping out of her. She still didn't get it. The rain under her felt hot, that's all. I guess our brains tell us lies when death is near. Because the pain wasn't a punch, and the hot water wasn't rain. A sniper's bullet had blown a hole through the center of her chest.

She died not knowing who she was.

I close my eyes and step back.

"What's wrong?" he says.

Microphone feedback squeals across the gym. A few hundred people wince and groan. Someone screams dramatically and someone laughs too loudly.

"I'm fine," I say, trying to smile. The hand on my waist moves to my shoulder, almost to my neck.

"Don't—" he begins.

The DJ's voice scratches over the speakers. "I don't normally do this, but . . . we have a special request tonight. This is going out from Mrs. North to Nina. Mommy misses you."

I pull away from Noah like he shoved me. Laughter echoes around us. His face mirrors my own—open mouth, wide eyes. It doesn't make sense. Mrs. North is dead. And if she isn't, she wouldn't be dedicating a song to someone named Nina.

Noah's face changes from shock to doubt. "Did he . . . ?"

I nod. "He did."

It's quite possible a student with the last name North goes to this school. And it's possible her mom just requested a song for her. *Nina* is why I don't freak out completely; I don't know a Nina.

It has to be a coincidence.

It can't be a coincidence.

The new song starts up. The laughter fades and the dancing resumes.

I replay the words in my head.

Mrs. North to Nina.

Mommy misses you.

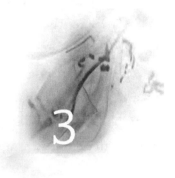

3

"What does it mean?" I say. My blood pounds off time with the music, two separate songs clashing in my ears.

Believing in coincidences is not something any of us can afford. So that would mean the creators found us. But it doesn't explain a weird DJ request. Unless they're trying to unnerve us or flush us out.

Noah shakes his head. "This isn't right." He spins a slow circle; I follow his gaze, checking the double door exits on every wall. No commotion, no abnormal movement besides awkward dancing.

Next I stand on tiptoe and scan the crowd, searching for the rest of our team.

"Where is everyone?" Noah says.

The song has a fast beat, and bodies are bobbing and swaying through our field of vision. My mind is still caught on *Nina*. It could be some kind of code. For what, I don't know. And the phrase *Mommy misses you* was deliberate too, like a code.

"There!" Noah says, pointing toward the DJ's booth in the corner, where the top of Sequel's head is visible.

I follow the path Noah carves through the crowd. We stop in front of the booth.

Sequel faces away from us, head down. Peter stands a few feet away, like he's afraid to get closer. Rhys is moving toward us, trying to slip around a mass of dancers.

"She just shut down," Peter says, yelling over the music. "After the request she just walked away from me. I found her like this."

No one speaks. The DJ is looking at something on his cell phone. Peter points at him, and Rhys nods, then tries to push through a wall of dancers. When I look back, the DJ is already gone.

"You okay?" I say.

"I'm fine," Sequel says, still facing away from me. I don't relax.

Peter says, "I'll help Rhys trap the DJ. We need to leave, now."

Before I can say splitting up isn't a good idea, Peter is gone.

Noah edges around Sequel and leans over, peering up into her face. "What's wrong?" he says.

I put a hand on Sequel's shoulder, and everything changes.

My feet are off the ground. It takes a full second to realize what happened—she spun in a blur and delivered a palm strike to my sternum. The stunned feeling fades, replaced by the no-breath feeling. None. My back hits the floor and I slide away from Sequel, tripping people with my shoulders. They cry out and thump against the gym floor around me. Through tear-blurred eyes, I see Noah crumpled against the wall, blood smeared on his lips and under his nose.

Helpful hands grab me under the arms and lift me up. People ask me questions but it's just background noise. Air comes in hot thimbles; I can't take a full breath. Sequel studies me with narrowed eyes, like she's wondering how I got all the way over here. Because this is a mistake. She reacted badly, that's all.

No one dances on this side of the gym, but the music still plays. *Everyone, everyone is the same,* the singer sings.

Then I smell it. There is no mistake.

The scent of roses.

"No!" I extend my hand, palm out, like I can push the psychic energy away, or back into Sequel's brain. But nothing can stop her. This is what all of us were designed to do—terrify people until they can't function, until they go insane.

The panic catches. First the students around me go rigid. A girl's scream pierces the music. People react in different ways to the energy. Someone falls hard; I feel a thump through the floor. Some don't do anything at all, frozen in time. Everyone perks up as if some important announcement has come over the PA. The rose scent thickens. I step forward as Noah is getting to his feet, preparing to lunge. Sequel spins hard and tight, leg rising, and kicks Noah in the chest. He slams into the wall again.

The scent is choking now. I can feel her fear-waves lapping at my brain. "Sequel!" I say. "Miranda!" A last-ditch effort to wake her from whatever spell she's under. The waves have no effect on me, but I feel them. She isn't stopping. Her eyes are screwed shut, nose crinkled. That's it. I charge forward—

As everyone loses their sanity completely.

Feet pound, like they did during the pep rally a few days ago. Shoulders and elbows and knees slam into me, carrying me away from Sequel like a tide. A shoulder spins me to the ground, someone steps on my ribs, and a girl's heel stabs at my kidney. I can't breathe again.

Students groan and yell out as they bottleneck at the exits behind me. The only way to help them is to stop Sequel. I pull myself into a ball as more feet kick my spine and shoulders. My skin throbs at each impact point. Another heel catches the strap on my dress and tears it. I place both hands flat on the floor and push myself upright with all my strength, sticking my elbows out to block the crowd. I keep my eyes off their stricken faces. Soon their fear will turn to pure madness—no thought—unless I make her *stop*.

I surge forward as Sequel pushes through a side exit. I almost go after her alone, but Noah staggers to his feet again, reaching for me with one hand.

I grab his outstretched fingers and pull him along. "Come on!"

"What's *wrong* with her?" he says, blood dripping from his nose.

We push through double doors into the cafeteria. They slam shut behind us, but I can still hear the stampede—a thumping bass from the music and feet. I imagine broken bones and trampled bodies, things I saw on the streets of Cleveland last summer, just twelve miles north of us. All because we decided to play at a normal life. Our classmates are paying the price.

"Mir!" Noah says, pulling up short. Sequel watches us from the other end of the cafeteria, where the main hallway begins. Her face is completely blank and emotionless . . . until her mouth drops open and her eyes go wide.

"Don't follow me! Don't follow—"

She cuts off midsentence, then shakes her head as if to clear it. The shock on her face is replaced with a close-lipped smile I've never seen her make before.

Then she's gone. I kick off my shoes in two steps. The red heels skitter over the tile. Noah loosens his striped tie and pulls it over his head. A memory belonging to the Miranda before me surfaces, one of *Sifu* Phil telling us neckties are a good way to get strangled.

Noah and I reach the end of the cafeteria in time to see Sequel disappear down an adjacent hallway.

"Be careful," Noah says between breaths. I think he's saying it for both of us. Because this is wrong. Chasing Sequel is wrong. I feel pulled in two directions—half of me wants to go back and get the others, because we have no idea what we're dealing with. I'm wearing a silky red dress and Noah sports a black dress shirt and pants. But if I go back, it might take too long to find them, and leaving Noah to pursue Sequel alone is not an option. We slow until our footsteps are just whispers on the rough carpet.

We round the corner into the next hallway. A door up ahead sighs shut, then clicks. The hallway stretches past it for the length of the school, lit only in intervals. Sequel couldn't hide in the sectors of darkness; I'd be able to see her outline against the light.

Noah touches my shoulder. "Go back," he whispers. "Grab everyone else. I'll watch the door."

"What if she comes out?"

"She won't."

"What if she does?"

"Miranda, *she won't*. It's Sequel."

"You go."

We stare at each other for a few seconds. We know each other well enough to know neither is going to budge.

He sighs. "Then I go in first."

"No objections here." Only because it's a compromise, and because Sequel likes Noah more than she likes me. He opens the door and plunges into the darkness and I'm a step behind him. My fingers brush the wall until I feel the little nub of the light switch. I hear a wet *thunk*, and then a splash, like someone kicked over a can of paint. The fluorescents hiss to life in the ceiling, revealing a science lab. Black worktables are covered in scales and beakers and unlit Bunsen burners.

Noah stands still in front of me. A jagged splash of red at his feet.

My eyes ache as they adjust to the light. The air is gone from my lungs and I'm frozen in the doorway, wondering what the red on the floor means.

Sequel sits on the second table in front of us, a sword resting across her lap. The blade is red and wet along its length. She looks at me like a robot. No soul. Wait, there—a spark behind her eyes as they narrow. It's almost familiar.

"You can say good-bye," she says. "I'll wait."

Noah turns around and his foot slips in the blood and he

falls against the first table. It's solid, stacked with drawers holding more lab equipment. Noah's right hand clutches his throat. His throat and chin are wet and red. He slumps down and I fall with him, on my knees, in his blood.

"Let me see, let me see." I'm outside myself, hovering over us both. It's a movie now. It's not real.

I peel his fingers back gently and see. A single cut. So deep. His blood pumps out in a rhythm. I clamp my palm over it and feel his blood surging out in a warm, hard jet. His eyes are wet with tears. I can't even lie to him. I can't tell him it's okay. My right hand shakes. I place it over my left, where the blood runs between my fingers. "Oh, Noah . . ." *Say something else. Say something important. Show him he isn't alone, that he never was.*

"Sorry, Mir." His voice is a choked whisper, almost too quiet to hear. He coughs once, and blood flecks my face. Hot pinpricks on my cheeks.

"No no. Don't be sorry."

He turns his head left, then right. He's trying to shake his head, but it doesn't look right. I unclench my hand and press it to his cheek. It won't stop shaking.

"Is it really you?" he says, quiet and slow.

It takes me a second before I realize what he's asking. *Is it really me?* He had his suspicions then, that I wasn't the girl whose life he erased.

"It's me. It's me."

I don't even have to think about it. I can't tell him the truth. Not now. It would change nothing.

"You forgive me?"

"Yes." I forgive him on behalf of the girl who came before.

His blood is foamy red and he's asking for forgiveness. That's what he cares about right now. At the end. Because this is the end. A strange sound comes out of my throat. I don't want to cry. I want to see clearly, and I want to hear him, hear everything he says and imprint it in my mind. Remember it for as long as I live.

"It was wrong," he says.

"No."

"I just loved you so much," he says. His eyes are lidded. His face is bloodless. His words sting and make me feel unworthy. Because I'm not the girl he loved. His words don't belong to me.

"I know. I loved you too."

"Still do? You can lie."

"Yes." And I do love him. Maybe I always did. It took the end to bring it out of me. I love Peter, but I love Noah. Without Noah, I wouldn't be here. I'd be growing in a tank, forgotten, waiting to be sold as a weapon. "Not lying," I say.

His pulse is weak against my palm. His blood covers me, already cooling outside his body.

"Don't forget me."

"I couldn't."

His eyelids droop. I read a word on his lips. Two words. There's no sound, but I understand. *Kiss me*, he says.

I lean forward and press my lips to his cold, bloodless ones. I feel tension in his lips for a second as he kisses back. Then they go slack. I press my forehead to his and the tears won't be stopped this time. They fall from my cheeks to his and mix with his blood.

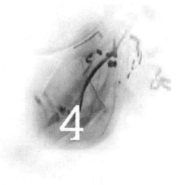

4

S oon this cold, black void fills me up. It's weird to think of it that way, a void filling you, but it does. I guide Noah to his side, gently, and run my hand over his hair.

I speak to the room. My voice is dead and flat. "Are you still here?"

My voice comes back to me. "I am."

I stand up in Noah's blood. It's lukewarm between my toes. I suddenly feel sick, and my throat flexes in a half gag. Sequel sits on the table, in the lotus position, sword across her lap. I step back, out of Noah's blood. My bare feet leave bright red prints on the white linoleum. My arms are glazed from fingernails to elbows.

"Where did you get . . . ?" I lick my lips. Taste more blood. I can't speak. I have so many things to say.

"The sword?"

She looks at Noah's feet poking out from behind the table. I want to cut her eyes out of her head. She doesn't get to look at him.

"Sequel hid it in this room," she says. "She has one in the auditorium too. I guess she didn't trust this place." I should have expected this; she wasn't the only one. I also hid a pack of throwing knives in the library on the second day. But right now they're one floor and several hundred feet away.

"Nina."

Nina doesn't blink. "My name, yes."

The message changed her in some way, brought out some new personality. I know Sequel as well as I know myself, because we came from the same place. This person isn't her.

I sway in place, lost. Nina stares at me, unblinking. If we share the same mind, then she knows I'm not going to walk away. I'm not going to quit until one of us is dead. So I get on with it. I step forward to the nearest table and grab a beaker. I throw it like a baseball. Her sword blurs in front of her face, and the glass shatters. Shards pepper her chest and fall around her. Another beaker follows, then a scale. She bats them all away, legs still folded under her.

The void inside me doesn't last. Something else seeps in, red and hot.

And once the rage starts it doesn't stop. I want to temper it somehow, maintain control and precision, but I can't.

Anger has no place in battle. Sifu Phil's words, echoing from some long-ago lesson I never attended. *It may grant you strength, but the serene warrior is the survivor. Do not mistake serene for passionless. You must temper your feelings like a blade.*

I temper my feelings like a blade.

Nina doesn't flinch as I come at her, and why should she? She's armed and I'm not. She hops off the table and lunges forward with her sword. She stops with the point touching my throat, tenting the skin inward. I could knock it away, or step back, but I don't. She would've killed me already if she wanted to, while I hovered over Noah, and I don't know why she hasn't. Why spare me then, and why spare me now? This is me tempering the blade.

I hold my hands out, showing my empty, bloodstained palms. Daring Nina to finish me. I want her to, I think. Then I won't have to feel what I'm feeling.

The pressure feels good in a strange way; it gives me something to focus on. I lean in to the point and my skin breaks. Hot blood rolls into the hollow of my throat. Her eyes narrow, and I use the moment to bat the sword away and grip her throat.

I squeeze and watch her eyes turn red and her mouth open and close. I pry the sword from her fingers with my other hand. She gives it up too easily, and alarm bells go off in my head. She grabs the bottom of the hilt, under my fingers, and pulls hard. A small knife drops out. It was hidden inside the hilt. Stupid me—so much for a tempered blade. I don't deserve to win.

She rips the tiny knife across my left forearm, the one trying to crush her trachea. My arm numbs instantly. My fingers loosen even though I try to squeeze tighter. Blood wells in the cut and rolls down the curve of my arm. I bring my forearm to my face and take a step back, almost falling. My legs are numb too.

I look up.

Two images dance around and meld into Nina's smiling face.

"Poison," I slur. I can barely stand. I wait for Peter and Rhys to burst through the door, but they don't. I'm alone.

"Sit down for the next part," Nina says. "Don't hurt yourself falling down."

My steps turn shaky as the poison spreads through my body. The pool of Noah's blood splits into two crimson lakes, then snaps back to one. Another step. I use the table to guide me down. Doesn't matter, really. If I never wake up, I made enough mistakes to deserve it. The only thing keeping me conscious is the rest of Alpha team, just a few hundred feet away, oblivious to what's happening. They're looking for us, probably. I can't warn them. I can't even save myself.

I end up on my side, looking into Noah's eyes. They're blank and glazed, half shut. Just like mine.

A black wave crashes over me, blotting out the light.

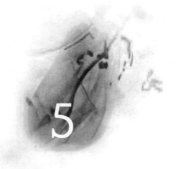

5

I wake up how I fell asleep—drugged, with my cheek against the floor.

My eyes won't focus no matter how hard I strain. Someone beats a war drum—*boom boom boom*. It takes me a second to realize it's just the blood in my ears. My left wrist is locked in a metal cuff as wide as my palm. It connects to a rusty chain looped around a thick iron pillar. The chain is locked to itself with a thick padlock. Seeing the chain and the pillar gives me that trapped animal feeling. The drug makes it worse.

I close my eyes for a full minute, trying to will the drug out of my system. When I open them, two vibrating images of the ceiling meld into one. Cobwebs cover the exposed support beams. The concrete floor is cracked and canted in places. The air smells like wet mattresses. I sit upright and wrap my arms around my knees. Blood rushes to my head, and suddenly I feel a bruise on my right cheek, the scarred one. I focus on the pain. I don't know where I am.

Breathe.

I'm wearing my homecoming dress. Blood stains the front.

My hands shake and I shut my eyes. Tears leak out and roll down my cheeks, and there's nothing I can do to change what happened. Nothing. My throat makes a high sound I can't stop. I can't breathe. I don't want to breathe. I want to stay here and suffocate so I can see Noah's face again.

I explode upright and put one foot flat on the pillar. I wrap the chain around both hands and pull back with everything I've got, picturing Noah on his side. The chain bites into my fingers. The links scrape and slide on the padlock. I strain so hard, capillaries burst in my eyes, but I don't stop. I can't stop. If I stop, that's it. I'll never have the strength I do at this moment, right now.

I stop.

And collapse, spent, heaving, sick. The chain claps back to the floor. My palms are orange-red, smeared with rust and dried blood. I rub them down the front of my dress, but it doesn't come off. I rub and rub, and it just smears the blood deeper into my skin.

I sniff a few times and pretend this isn't the end. I just have to try harder. In a few minutes, I'll give it another shot. Yeah, I'll just rest for a minute. Maybe I can climb the pillar and try to break through the wooden support beam at the top. It would help if there was some other noise down here, maybe a faulty furnace ticking and coughing, so I could hear something other than my frantic heart and raspy breath.

Seconds pass, and reality sets in. The others will have to fight on without me. I think I'm saddest about that part most of all.

I stand up for another try anyway. As I do, a slow clap comes from the darkest corner of the room. I spin around and almost trip myself on the chain.

"A for effort. But a D for logic. Even a Rose isn't strong enough to break iron."

Nina steps out of the darkness. She has replaced her dress with one of our formfitting suits. The suit is layered in black scales, like a fish. It covers her fingers and toes and ends below her jaw. Her short, clinging black hair looks like part of the suit, a cowl.

Her right hand holds a gun.

I put a hand against the wall, prepared to fight if I can.

Something changes from one second to the next—her eyes. Not blank and soulless, but horrified. She looks down at the gun in her hand, like *Where did this come from?*

She's Sequel again. Not Nina—whoever Nina is. There is no faking the revulsion on her face.

"I feel her inside me, you know?" She shakes the words out. Her eyes are shiny with tears.

Whatever she has to say, I don't care. I tell myself that because I want it to be true.

"Feel who?" My voice is dry.

She squeezes her eyes shut, quaking. A tear wells in her right eye, slips down the side of her nose. "I'm so sorry, Miranda."

"Feel who, Sequel? Who?"

"Nina."

"Who is Nina?"

"North Iteration 9-A. I can feel her."

"What is that?"

"I don't *know.*"

She grips the side of her head and squeezes so hard I wince. She's only five feet away. A little closer and I could reach out and grab her.

"She keeps making me watch when she takes over, and I—I don't know. When I cut . . ."

When I cut Noah.

"Don't cry for him," I say. She isn't allowed to feel anything. I don't care who takes over and makes her watch. I don't care I don't care.

Her eyes flare red, literally. She's not wearing her contacts. *"Listen to me.* There is more to this. She's in control. There's a plan, Miranda. A plan. And I can't stop her—"

"Why am I here? What do you *want*?"

"Because she wants to use you. She brought you here. But she let her guard down and now I'm here and it's really me. It wasn't me before, please. Believe me." Her next words are garbled from her crying. *"I didn't want him to die."*

I believe her. My left hand balls into a fist until a knuckle pops. Can I really hurt her when she's Sequel? If what she says is true, she's trapped inside. She's a prisoner like me, but worse. I still own my body. If she drifts too close, it would be my responsibility to end her before she causes more damage.

"Did she kill Noah?" I say. "Was that Nina?"

"Yes . . ."

I visualize how we found Sequel on the operating table in Key Tower. She had scraps of memories from the previous Miranda, like me. Mrs. North must've put whatever North Iteration 9-A is inside of her then. Hidden the identity underneath Sequel. Then the DJ's message activated it somehow, the same way Mrs. North recalled memories in me last summer.

Mrs. North showed me the truth, that I wasn't the Miranda everyone had grown up with, but a replacement. A fake.

Sequel is still holding the gun at her side.

"This thing she wants me to do. She wants me to gather something, or lead something, I don't know. *I don't know.* I can't see much. But it's bad. It's really bad. She wants me to find the other creators and kill them. Then she wants to . . ."

"Stop," I say. "She *wants* you to do it, or she's taking over and doing it herself? Which is it?"

"It's *both*. Sometimes we're both in here and I can't tell where I start and she ends."

"What does she want you to do?"

She closes her eyes. Her hands curl into fists. "She's coming."

"Give me the gun."

She considers the gun again, like she forgot she was holding it. My heart pounds so hard I can barely hear her. "She wants me to gather the eyeless. To open the way for them. To—to lead them. I don't know what it *means*."

I just stare at her, feeling how Noah's dried blood is thicker in the creases of my palms. Rimmed under my fingernails and cuticles, like badly applied nail polish.

Save your words, I want to say. *I don't care. Leave me alone.*

But part of me can't help but listen.

Eyeless.

Open the way.

Lead them.

Them, Mrs. North said in the memory. This is it. These are the monsters we've been waiting for. It has to be.

"What are the eyeless? Is it some kind of weapon? Sequel, look at me!"

She looks. Her eyes are bloodshot, and she keeps shaking her head. "No. No. No. Miranda."

I push off the wall and stretch to the end of my chain, until it bites into my wrist. The cuff pulls the skin; the cut on my arm opens again. Warm blood rolls down my arm and inside the cuff.

"Give me the gun!"

She has something else attached to her hip. A key. She pries it off and holds it up, a gun in one hand and a key in the other. "I don't want to die," she says. "You're going to kill me."

"We can help you! We can...." It's a lie, and I know it. My hands are sticky with Noah's blood. Noah is dead because of her. There will be no helping her. But if what she says is true, then Sequel is innocent. It's the identity inside her that's guilty.

Her eyes blink rapidly, then freeze. Looking right at me. Nina's eyes. "I don't need help," she says.

Nina takes a step back and shakes her head. Her smooth face breaks again, crinkling. "Noah..." she whispers.

I wiggle my wrist inside the cuff, which my blood has

lubricated, but it's still too tight to slip my hand through. I fold my thumb across my palm and pull with everything in me, until my eyes see little white zooming stars.

I give up.

She drops the key. It bounces twice, ringing on the concrete floor.

"I want to live," she says quietly, as Sequel once again. Ashamed. I can't blame her, really. She wants to live. Would I be strong enough to kill myself if I knew I had some hidden, malign aspect of my personality? Someone guiding me, making me do things I didn't want to do?

Taking me over?

I don't know.

"I'll find another way," she says, wiping her cheeks with her fingertips. "I can force her out. I can do it."

I sway in place, swallowing against the urge to vomit. The key is too far away. "What if you can't? She's going to use you. *Hey.*" She lifts her shame-filled eyes to me. "She'll use you to *kill us.* Like Noah."

Sequel turns away. She sticks the gun against her hip again.

"I'm going to come after you!" I scream at her. She walks up the steps, slowly, head down. "You should kill me!" Anything to make her come back. *Give me the gun. Give me the gun so I can stop whatever Nina makes you do.*

43

She says nothing, keeps climbing.

I lunge for the key and fall hard on my chest, gasping. My trembling fingers hover a few inches away. A door shuts upstairs. I stretch harder, moaning as the cuff cuts deeper into my wrist. Then I stop being brain-dead. I flip around and use my foot to pull the key to me. My feet are blood-spattered, like my hands. I was standing in Noah's blood.

I get the key and jam it into the lock. A twist, and the cuff pops open. I charge up the stairs into a home from the seventies. Everything is dressed in yellow and dust. Cupboards filled with cobwebs stand open. The front door squeals when I shove through. It's full dark outside, no stars. No moon. A cool autumn night, the night Noah died. The faint scent of roses is on the air, and I follow it over the damp backyard grass and up someone's driveway. My skin is colder in the unbloody places.

A man shouts to my left. I turn just in time to see Nina throw a man out of his tiny car. She slips behind the wheel, shuts the door, and takes off with squealing tires. I step into the street, and the headlights fill my eyes. The engine screams as Nina pushes the pedal to the floor. The car grows and grows until it's right in front of me, and I almost let it hit me, but at the last moment I leap straight up and tuck my legs and feel the car pass under me. The turbulent air tugs me back down. The blacktop pebbles bite into my toes, and I turn to watch the taillights shrink to red pinpricks. Five seconds later, Nina squeals around a corner and is gone.

My mind is blissfully blank until I picture Noah lying next to the table. Someone has found him by now; someone called for help even though they knew it was useless. Maybe they immediately searched for Peter and Rhys, or me and Sequel. Everyone saw the five of us together—another stupid move, even if we've only been in school a few weeks. I hope Peter and Rhys were smart enough to take off rather than get pulled into questioning by the police.

A thought strikes me like a bullet—I am a product of Mrs. North. She could've sewn some latent personality into my brain too. There could be a different North Iteration swimming inside me, waiting to hear a specific set of words or numbers. Then she'll surface, and I'll be a danger to everyone.

And whatever made Mrs. North so ruthless in the first place is inside of me too. I could become like her simply because we have the same DNA. Her blood, her exact blood, already flows through my veins.

It's not fair to Peter and Rhys. I try to imagine the things they'll say when they realize the implications. It makes me sick all over again.

Headlights swing down the quiet road. My breath fogs out. I must be some sight—a shivering girl in a bloody red dress.

The car stops like I knew it would. The driver gets out, some guy asking if I'm okay. I'm not okay. I tell him I need his car. He says, "What?" I sweep his legs out from under him and get inside and close the door.

The radio plays pop music. The clock says Noah died two hours ago.

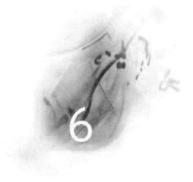

6

I find the highway and drive south toward the suburbs. We moved out of Rhys's luxury condo when we realized our funds weren't unlimited. The three-bedroom apartment we share is cramped, but home enough.

I look for the aqua Dodge Caravan Rhys bought for five hundred dollars, but it's not in the usual space. Then I see it, tucked away in the back. They're home.

One of our neighbors, Mrs. Prenelow, sees me wearing my bloody dress, but I'm too raw to care. She's half blind anyway. I nod at her, and her eyes follow me up the stairs. I have a feeling it'll be the last time I see her.

The carpet in our outer hallway is stained brown with

years. I smell cigarettes burning in the next unit over, two boys in their twenties who play video games until four in the morning. I put my ear to our door and listen, but hear nothing.

It'll be easier to see Peter before Rhys.

Peter first, because no matter what he'll hear me out before judging my stupid decision to take on Nina alone rather than regrouping. That's just how he works. He's like the human embodiment of justice or something.

At least Rhys is likely to focus his anger on who killed Noah, not on me.

I knock, and the door whips open two seconds later.

Peter stands in the doorway. His face is hard. "Where was our first kiss?" he demands.

A slap across the face. I stand there for two whole seconds. "The bathroom stall, the night before the dry run." My answer doesn't prove who I am. I've been gone for over two hours. For all they know, the creators picked me up and stole my memories and replaced me with a new clone. I guess I pass, despite that.

Peter wraps his arms around me, holding me up. I give him my weight gladly. Rhys comes over and stands there for a moment, then he hugs both of us. We stand like that for a few seconds.

"Who killed him?" they eventually ask.

When I tell them, they believe me, but they don't understand.

❀   ❀   ❀

We do everything at once. I throw a sandwich down my throat and they finish putting on their armor, and then I get in the shower. I have to wash the blood off. Our place might be compromised, so we need to leave pretty much immediately. Not to mention every minute adds to Nina's lead. I turn the water on hot enough to melt skin. I peel the dress off; it pulls at my stomach, where the blood dried. Then I stand under the flow and watch the water shade from brown to red, to pink, to clear.

I leave the door open so they can hear me. I tell them everything. I hear them running up and down the hallway while I talk, searching the places we've stashed weapons or resources like bottled water and packaged food. Anything for an extended trip.

I tell them I was kept alive because Nina, or Mrs. North, or whoever the hell, wanted to use me for something. I don't bring up that it's possible I'm as dangerous as Nina. I wait for Peter to draw the same conclusion, but I can't tell if he does. It makes my skin itch. I *want* him to realize it so I don't have to tell him.

"I found Noah," is all Peter says when I get out of the shower.

"I lost the DJ," is all Rhys says, and he sounds so mad

at himself, I'm surprised he hasn't punched holes in the wall.

On the way back from the bathroom, I stop in the room Rhys shared with Noah. I don't know why. Noah's bed is against the wall. The sheets are twisted from when he rolled out of it yesterday morning, before we all went to get breakfast at a diner. Sequel had come out of the shower wearing the same green shirt I was wearing. Neither of us had budged. "Fine, I'll change," she said, but I told her it didn't matter. We were supposed to be twins anyway. That wasn't even twenty-four hours ago. I hear the sound Noah's blood made in the dark, paint spilling over the floor. *Don't forget me.*

Rhys is cleaning his gun at the low dresser. He's scrubbing the barrel so hard the lubed metal slips out of his hand, and he catches it and keeps scrubbing with the same motion. Peter is rooting around for something in Noah's closet.

Rhys looks up from his disassembled gun. "Hey."

I blink.

"We need to get to Noah," I say. "I want his memories." I don't want to forget him.

Peter steps out of the closet. "What are you thinking?"

"Noah spent so much time with Sequel. Maybe she said something, or he saw something that will give us a clue." But that means we have to get to his body now, before his brain cells break down too much. It might already be too late to copy his memories.

If it works, I'll have his personality in a box. I don't want that kind of responsibility. I don't want to be the keeper of his identity.

"I can't think of another lead," Peter says, staring at the floor, eyes unfocused. "I don't know where to look for her."

"Good plan," Rhys says, looking a little pale at the thought.

I go to my room and slip into my armor and feel better immediately. The invisible seam in the back closes to the top of my spine, and the lightweight material shifts and hugs the contours of my body. The painkilling system built into the armor's lining cools the burn of my cut forearm. I feel safe and secure with my second skin.

Next come my sword and revolver. I used to look at my weapons with a kind of reverence, but now I know they're just tools. My sword is straight and light and narrow, and my gun holds six bullets. The gun sticks to my left hip. The sword, Beacon, sticks to my back.

While Rhys packs the memory machine, I find Peter in his room looking out the window.

We're alone for a moment. I have to share my fear. If I don't tell him, it's going to burn me hollow from the inside out.

I step inside and shut the door behind me. "What if I'm like her?" I say, no preamble.

He doesn't reply, but his shoulders tense slightly. *Please say something. Tell me I'm an idiot, that the very idea is absurd.*

"I could be like Nina," I say again to clarify.

He turns around. "I know."

A terrible second passes.

"It doesn't matter, though," he says.

"Oh really? How do you figure? I was born a few days before Sequel, and Mrs. North wasn't rushed with me. She could've put *anything* inside my head. Why would she do something to Sequel and not me?"

Peter swallows, and his eyes flit away for a second, but he forces them back to me. "I agree it's possible, maybe even likely."

"So you need to make a decision."

He shakes his head, just an inch. "No, I don't. I'm not going to worry about something we have no control over. We're not leaving you here. We're not splitting up. So it doesn't really matter, does it?" He closes the distance between us and grabs the tops of my arms and squeezes gently. "If something happens —if you change—we'll deal with it along the way."

"That's stupid. Tycast didn't make you leader to put your team at risk." The words come out heavy, on the verge of a sob.

Dr. Tycast, the man who raised us, put Peter in charge because he's the best of us. He's not getting upset over what-ifs like I am. I imagine the hidden Iteration inside me laughing, waiting.

"You think I want to lead? I didn't ask Tycast to pick me. I didn't. Noah wanted it more. And you know what Tycast told me once? That he picked me because I didn't want it. I just wanted to be part of the team. So don't think I'm going to stand here and tell the girl I love that, yeah, you're a risk, and yeah, I want you to leave. Because I don't. We need you, and you need us."

His words should make me feel better—I was counting on that—but they don't change the facts. I could run away. Let Peter and Rhys go on without me, instead of forcing them to make a choice.

Peter must see the possibility cross my face. "Don't even think about it," he says. "After everything, how could you think I'd let you get away?"

He pulls me forward and presses his lips to my forehead. The feel of his kiss relaxes the knots in my muscles. Knots that reappear the second he pulls back. He walks out of the room, discussion over.

Sounds good on paper, but the possibility *will* linger in their minds. How can they possibly trust me, fully, the way they used to? They can't.

I don't let it go, but I push it down. For now.

In the main room, Rhys has the memory band in the duffel slung over his shoulder. He cracks a bottle of water and drinks the whole thing. "Thirty seconds," Peter calls from another room. I hear the metal scrape of a gun being assembled.

Rhys hands me a bottle of water. "What are you thinking about?"

I'm thinking about when Noah used the last of the peanut butter and put the empty jar back on the shelf. And I called him an asshole—over peanut butter. He apologized, and I said there was no excuse, none, because he *knew* the peanut butter was empty. He'd scraped it out himself. He didn't try to fight me on it, just looked remorseful and walked away. That was last week. I got mad at him over peanut butter, and now he's on a cold slab, bloodless, unable to know or care about anything. I'm sorry about yelling at him, and he'll never know that.

Then I think about the next day, when I passed by the open bathroom door and Noah and Sequel had their faces pressed together. I only saw it out of the corner of my eye. I didn't slow down, but I heard their mouths break away after I passed them. It had been a kiss. I went to my room and sat on the bed and tried to understand what I was feeling. Sad, a little, but less guilty since Noah was finally happy.

"Nothing," I say.

After a quick weapons check, I stand in the doorway, taking in what was once our home. We'll probably never come back here.

Peter and Rhys are in the hallway.

"Come on, Miranda," Rhys says softly.

I close the door and lock it.

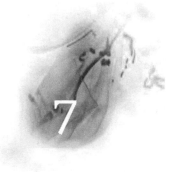

7

While I'm driving us back to the school, Peter pulls out a pill bottle and shakes three tiny black pills into his palm. It's just before midnight, and the roads are empty and dark.

"We need to swallow these," he says, handing one to me and one to Rhys.

"Why?" I say.

"Because I don't have the injector to put them inside us. It broke. This will let us track one another."

"I don't know," I say. My first thought is that if I turn into someone else, I'll know how to find them easily.

Peter's eyes are a little shiny, but he might just be tired. He wipes at them. "Well, I do know. I couldn't find you before. Now I can find you."

"They won't be useful for long...." Rhys says.

Peter shrugs. "There's more in the bottle. Take them."

So we do. Peter gives us handheld readouts that show how far away each tracker is, and in what direction and elevation. I put mine in one of the little pouches on my waist, among the speedloaders for my revolver.

We get to the school at 12:09, which means Nina's been on the loose for over two hours. Either that's a huge head start, or she's had time to plan a strike against us.

Police cruisers sit bumper to bumper along the front curb, glowing under the parking-lot lights. One ambulance sits at the front of the line. I know who it's for; Noah's death is the unconnected one. He wasn't trampled or crushed in the gym. I can't imagine what theories the detectives are tossing around. *He was a new kid,* someone will say. *New this year.* They'll pull up his records and see that his emergency contact info leads nowhere. *Who was this kid?* they'll ask. *Who did he belong to?*

I park way in the back, hidden behind student cars left overnight. The buzz of a news helicopter overhead gives me a headache.

The students must be coherent by now, the psychic energy having dissipated hours ago. Right away, people will see the connection to last summer, when Roses like us used their powers on the downtown area. Both attacks involved terror and panic without an obvious stimulus. I try to imagine how my ex-classmates will put the fear into words. That kind of fear is something I can't biologically experience. I remember watching a news special after the attack on downtown. They interviewed people who said things like, "I can't remember what I was afraid of, I was just afraid. It was beyond fear. I really can't say what it was." I can—it was us.

I squeeze the steering wheel, unclench my aching jaw.

Peter takes my hands off the wheel and puts them in my lap, then lays his hand on top. His is cool and dry and sure. Steady.

"Relax," he says, then points through the windshield. "Here they come."

I follow his gaze to the main entrance. Two cops and two paramedics wheel a gurney down the sidewalk, through pools of brightness and shadow. A white sheet covers the outline of Noah on his back. We're far away, but I can make out the red blotch where the sheet touches his neck.

I wonder if I'm going to cry again, but I don't feel anything. Just hollow. It's nice.

"Want me to drive?" Peter says.

"I got it."

"Want *me* to drive?" Rhys says.

"I said I got it." If I'm not okay enough to drive, we have a problem.

I watch them load the bag into the back of the ambulance. The doors slam, like sealing a tomb. The ambulance pulls away, no lights, no siren.

I put the van into gear and follow it.

The ambulance goes straight to the Cuyahoga County Coroner's Office. No one spoke during the ride because there is nothing to say. I park on the side. The building is white, four stories, and lacking any sinister characteristics. It doesn't look like it houses the bodies of those who've died suspiciously.

I watch the paramedics pull Noah from the ambulance and wheel his gurney through double doors.

I check the clock above the radio. 12:39. I lost Nina almost three hours ago now.

"They'll put him in the cooler and do an autopsy later," I say. The phrase *put him in the cooler* makes me sick. I can't believe I said it like that.

"The cooler will slow his decomp," Rhys says.

"Thank you, Dr. Rhys," Peter says.

"Doesn't matter," I say. "We'll give the paramedics ten minutes to put him there; then we go in. Good plan?"

"Decent enough," Rhys says.

Peter nods. He closes his eyes and settles into the seat, meditating.

Enough time passes and we get out of the Caravan, looking less than surreptitious in our scaly armor. None of us thought to bring over-clothes, but I guess we had our minds on other things. Rhys passes me the duffel bag that contains the machine. I try to take it, but he holds on to the strap.

"You sure you want Noah's memories swimming around in your head?" he says.

Not when he says it like that. But we need a clue, and there are none. The way he says it, I know he must be thinking the same thing. Noah knew Sequel, not Nina, and there may be no clues present in his memories. But I don't know where else to look.

And Noah's words, *Don't forget me*, still ring in my ears. I don't want to forget him. If someone has to sift through his memories, it's going to be me. Not that I could say that without feeling stupid. I can already hear Rhys's retort—*I don't think he meant remember him literally, Mir.* And he'd be right.

We go through the doors like we own the place, which, in a way, we do. No one here can stop us. The hallways are white and bright and sterile. Cold. We march down them in a loose triangle, Peter leading the way.

Someone shouts behind us, "Hey. Hey!"

I spin around, hands reaching for my weapons. A stout man in a blue uniform with a shiny silver badge stands in a doorway, hand on the doorknob, other hand on his holstered pistol. Just a few strides away.

His revolver is halfway off his leg when I do what Alpha team swore never to do, if we could help it. I release some of the tension that's always present in my brain, letting some of my energy escape in the smallest wave, just enough to get his hand off the gun. It hurts and feels good at the same time. His eyes widen and his nostrils flare; his mouth drops open.

"Miranda!" Peter says behind me.

I ignore him and close the distance to the guard, then grab a fistful of his shirt and twist, pulling him to me. I make my voice hard as rock. "Take us to the cooler."

The guard nods rapidly, eyes crinkling and swelling with tears. "Yes ... please ..." I feel him tremble through my closed fist. He's on the verge of screaming, or fainting, or both.

I let go of his shirt and grab his arm, which is already a little damp with sweat. "Lead us."

He starts off, breathing heavily and dragging me along. Peter and Rhys have nothing to say. The scent of roses—a weird side effect of our psychic power—is already fading. Maybe it wasn't the right call, but there's no use second-guessing it now.

Peter and Rhys lag behind.

"Come *on*," I say. The guard pulls me around a corner.

"How about a heads-up next time?" Peter says when they catch up.

"Heads-up on a snap decision? You got it."

Rhys snickers quietly.

Straight ahead is a big steel door with a pull handle. I know what it is before the guard says, "Here. Here."

I release the guard's arm. Rhys grabs his shoulders, spins him around, and hunches to look into his face. "Where's the nearest closet?"

"There's one in the next office...."

Rhys plucks the radio and gun off the guard's belt and turns him in the right direction. "I want you to go there and shut yourself in, and don't come out for an hour. Got it? Or... bad things will happen."

The guard nods and shuffles away, keys jangling on his belt.

Rhys turns back to me and Peter. "Who knew the fearful were so impressionable?"

We don't laugh, because it isn't really a joke. A few moments pass outside the big steel door. No one speaks. They have to be wondering if I'm strong enough. I know I am, but that doesn't mean I want to go inside.

Peter touches my elbow lightly. "I want you to let me do it. I don't know what absorbing all those memories will do to you."

If some latent personality wakes up inside me, would they have access to whatever I download from Noah? This is an unnecessary risk, and yet . . . I don't want anyone else to see. I don't want Peter or Rhys to see the memories Noah has of me. Who knows what happened between us over the years? I barely remember any of it. So I'm reckless, basically. Because I don't think that's a good enough reason to risk it, and yet I'm doing it anyway.

Instead of all that, I say, "I've downloaded memories from Rhys *and* Mrs. North. I'll be able to tell the difference between theirs and mine."

"This doesn't have to be your burden," Peter says.

He's right—it is a burden. It'll scald me in ways I can't anticipate, and I want it for the wrong reasons.

"This is my job," I say, hefting the duffel bag higher on my shoulder. "Unless that's an order?"

Several seconds pass. Then he shakes his head. "No."

I put my hand on the cold metal handle and yank the door open. Chilled, dry air spills out in a wave across my face. The lights inside are gray and bright and completely devoid of life, just like the rest of this place.

I step inside and shut the door behind me.

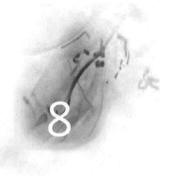

8

My suit fights the chill. I shiver for another reason.

The walls on my left and right are a grid of small rectangular doors, stacked three high. Behind them lie the dead. Bordering the walls are gurneys with sheets over them. The sheets are white silhouettes in the shapes of bodies, rounded near the heads, pointed at the feet.

I don't have to check each gurney; I see Noah right away. His gurney is against the far wall, the white sheet against the wall's puke-green tile. The bright red stain below the rise of his face has spread a little.

My breath comes in clouds of sour air. I watch Noah's sheet, expecting him to rise at any second. He'd pull the cover off and say "Surprise!" with that stupid grin. I'd punch him in the arm and he'd fake how much it hurt.

I blink.

The room is cold and dead. Noah is cold and dead. It's time to do my job. At Noah's gurney, I crouch and unzip the duffel and pull the memory band out.

My hand hovers over the sheet. I don't want to touch it. I don't want to pull it back and see his bloodless face. I close my eyes and breathe through my mouth, tasting the tang of antiseptic and the sweet smell of the newly dead. So strange, that cloying scent.

I stop stalling and pull the sheet off Noah. I crease it at the bottom of his ribs and force myself to look at his face. It's the way I remember it on the floor in the lab—cold and white and lifeless, with open eyes that will never see anything again. It's easy to see how deep the wound is now, the layers of skin and muscle Nina's sword cut through.

I grip the railing on his gurney and close my eyes.

Everyone is on a collision course with whatever is destined to kill them. Something will kill me one day, and it's out there now. Someone forged the blade that killed Noah. The edge met the soft flesh of Noah's neck, met the thin tubes that carried his blood underneath, all because I let him go first.

The tears on my cheeks are chilled, like my heart. I harden

myself to this and everything that comes next. Noah would want that.

I open my eyes and go to work, in the hopes that this is just one more step to making it all go away.

I have to lift his head up to secure the band. His hair is soft, and the dead weight of his head is the worst part. I close my eyes and slide it on by feel.

A small voice tells me this might not work, but I ignore it. I stomp the small voice under my armored feet. It has to work, or everything is for naught. I'll die before I let Nina win.

The memory band hums to life. I set the machine to start with Noah's newest memories; any clues to Nina's plans or whereabouts will be there.

The band purrs and clicks softly. My fingers trail down his forearm, grazing his wrist, then his palm. I almost hold his hand. Like that would make it easier for him. In truth, I can't stand the clammy feel of his skin.

Time passes too slowly, and the machine beeps now and again. Then the tiny readout on the side of his head says SCAN COMPLETE with four options underneath.

SCAN AGAIN | SAVE ALL | WIPE | NEW SUBJECT

I press SAVE ALL.

The band hums, saving whatever memories were intact in Noah's brain. Then it clicks and shuts down, the noise dying away like it's exhausted. I ease the band off Noah's face and settle it into the duffel.

Then I look at his eyes.

The irises are still brown, but a little pink, on their way to red, like mine. I use my fingers to close his eyes, but they ease open again. Staring. I try again and hold the lids down, and this time they stay closed enough. Cracked, but barely.

The sum of his life experience hangs off my shoulder, the heaviest weight I've ever carried.

I lay the sheet over him and turn around.

The door opens, but it's not Peter or Rhys. A woman in a white lab coat stands with a clipboard in both hands.

"You're not supposed to be here," she says. Her mouth opens and closes, brow crinkled as she takes in my armor. She's right. I'm not supposed to be here. Noah isn't supposed to be here, either.

She sees my eyes and visibly shrinks. I'm not wearing my contacts.

"What are you doing here?" she says.

I look at Noah one more time. The last time I'll ever see him. But I'm about to get closer to him than I ever was in life.

"Leaving," I say.

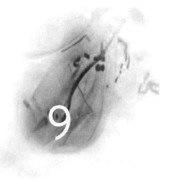

9

I tell the woman to stand in the cooler for five minutes, and
the look on her face tells me she'll comply. I shut the door
on her, then turn around to find Peter and Rhys standing
in front of me.

"Sorry, we thought it was better to hide," Rhys says.

"How'd it go?" Peter says as we start walking.

"Just wait," I say. The duffel is hot against my leg, and
I start worrying about stupid things. The machine could be
broken; he might have been dead too long; the memories could
be corrupted. A secret part of me wants the transfer to be a
failure—I won't have to see his memories, even if they might
help us. I won't have to see what it was like when he was still
alive, with thoughts of his own.

Outside, the cool early-fall air hits me, and I brace myself against the building with one hand. The fresh air is too much at once. I almost throw up, but don't. I just swallow a few times and look at the black sky. Peter and Rhys don't ask if I'm okay, which I'm grateful for. We just pile into the Caravan and drive away.

I sit in the backseat, on the bench Noah used to claim for his own. I look at the space next to me and remember him sitting here on our way to the dance, cracking his knuckles one by one, until Rhys told him to knock it off. His knuckle pops are like gunshots in my memory.

I pull out the memory band while Peter drives. I am hyper-aware that if this doesn't pan out, I've just wasted any chance we had at finding Nina.

Peter catches my eye in the mirror. "We have to sleep."

We've been up for around twenty hours, which isn't so bad, but it'll catch up with us soon. Right now I can't imagine sleeping. When I close my eyes, the background noise in my brain becomes louder.

"We can't go home," Rhys says.

"So find a place and park," I say.

Peter drives us somewhere, but I don't pay attention. I keep toying with the band, feeling its weight. Wondering what it's about to show me.

Eventually, Peter parks the van in some crowded parking lot and racks his seat back. Rhys does the same and says, "Good luck, Miranda." He probably falls asleep almost instantly.

Peter twists around on the seat. "If you insist on doing this, I'm staying up while you do."

I shake my head. "I won't be able to focus. Please, just trust me. Just..." I reach forward and touch his arm. After a moment, he places his hand over mine. "Just let me do this. I need you rested."

He doesn't say anything, no expression.

"Please," I say again. I'd do this alone if I could, in a dark room.

"Wake me when you're done, then," he says.

I give him the best smile I can. "Of course."

He watches me a second longer, always searching, then rolls over and lies still.

I could see so many things from Noah's life. I wonder what he'd say if he knew I was doing this. He'd probably start with NO.

The buttons glow a dull red in the dim light of the van. I press the one marked APPLY LAST SCAN and slide the band over my head. I hold my breath against the pain.

The memories come in a wave, too quick for me to grasp. I see images, not feelings. Noah brushes his teeth in the bathroom mirror. Rolls on the gym mat we put in the living room. Watches me and Sequel from the couch. Spars with Rhys, taking a blow to the ribs. The information rides thousands of microscopic tendrils directly into my brain tissue, where it becomes a tattoo. Mine, but not mine. Then the emotions catch up, and I fight the urge to lose myself.

Noah looks at me after we pull ourselves out of the river, soaking wet, having just evaded Beta team. Noah says goodbye to the Miranda before me, when he left her in Columbus with no memories. My own implanted memory of that moment rises up and I flicker back and forth between two sets of eyes, me looking at him without recognition, and him looking at me, eyes cracked and red with tears. Later, Noah is alone in the bathroom, crying. Noah kneels in front of the toilet, throwing up, regret burning his mind, wishing he hadn't taken her memories away, feeling his mistake with every cell.

The emotions connected to each memory threaten to overwhelm me, but I force myself to look at each one clinically. A slide show, nothing more. These feelings don't belong to me.

I want to look away. I want it to stop. But I can't and it doesn't.

As the memories pour into me, they truly become mine. I can pull them to the surface as easily as I can reference my own. I try to remember a time when Sequel was acting weird

or different. Maybe a private moment between them the rest
of us didn't see. If there's a clue, that's where I'll find it.

The rest of Noah's memories sit heavily in the back of my
mind, like a huge unread book I have to carry with me at all
times. They wait for me patiently.

But one comes to the surface, obeying my call.

I was so adamant about it before—no one could see Noah's
memories but me.

But now I regret not sharing the burden.

It starts with an argument and ends with something else.

I am me but not me. As each second passes, I'm less myself
observing Noah's memory and more Noah remembering his
own past.

Then I let go completely.

"You're a dick," Sequel says.

It feels like my chest cavity is filled with bees. Yes, bees. I
said the wrong thing again because I'm an idiot.

I called her Miranda. That doesn't sound too bad, but it is.
She's not Miranda. I've made her painfully aware of that fact.

"It was a reflex," I say.

"I'll make it easy for you," she says, not smiling. She stalks
into the bathroom and grabs a box of hair dye from under the

sink. The label says Raven Black. She finds scissors behind the mirror.

"You don't have to do that—"

"Don't watch me," she says, cutting off her auburn locks. They fall around her feet. Her movements are jerky as she tears open the box of dye.

I stop watching her, and she comes out a bit later with short black hair styled in what I later find out is called a pixie cut.

"Hey, looks good," I say as she passes right by me. She ignores me and leaves through the front door. This girl.

Naturally I follow her.

She takes the van, so I borrow a motorcycle from the parking lot. Not smart, but I would lose her otherwise. It's a black Yamaha R6 with a lot of miles.

I hang back and follow her for a half hour. She stops outside a squat brick building in the shitty part of town. Cheap jewelry stores and little quick marts jammed in with empty warehouses and grass-filled parking lots. No cars or people on the streets. I turn my headlight off and idle in the shadows between streetlights. After a full minute, Sequel turns down an alley next to the brick building. I hear the van shut off, so I kill the bike and sneak down the sidewalk, then pause at the mouth of the alley.

She stands in front of an old wooden door set into the

building. Without warning, she kicks it in and steps down into a basement. Makes total sense. Go to a strange building and kick the door in. It had a knob: I saw it. She didn't even check to see if it was unlocked. If she was meeting someone, she probably would've knocked.

She doesn't come out right away, so I sneak to the door, avoiding the garbage in the alley. She stands alone in a little brick room. Gray-green streetlight filters through the filthy windows. It smells like rat shit and mildew.

"I can't believe you followed me," she says.

I jump.

She turns around slowly. There's a different look in her eye. If she was mad at me before, she doesn't seem mad now. "Don't you have anything better to do with your time?"

"Not really," I say, trying to recover. I made absolutely no sound on my approach.

"Come here."

She has her hands out, grabbing for me.

My heart is pounding.

I go to her and take her hands, and she holds them both, and it's hard to swallow. I realize I want her very badly. I want her and I know that's weird, but I don't care.

She goes up on tiptoe and kisses me. It's a simple kiss. Our lips touch, nothing more. Hers are soft, mine are chapped.

"Was that okay?" she says.

74

I nod. Then I say, "Why did you come here?"

She shakes her head. She rises up again, but I turn my face from her kiss. I'm still stunned. I've felt these lips before, yet I haven't.

"I want to know," I say.

"It's stupid."

"I don't care."

"I'm just drawn to this place. How crazy does that sound?"

"Drawn here? You've come here before?" It strikes me how weird that is. She got mad, left, and drove to an empty room in a decrepit building.

She nods.

"Why?"

"I don't know."

"Okay, that's weird."

"Have you been with her?"

Boom, out of nowhere. My stomach twists. "What do you mean? Don't change the subject."

"You know exactly what I mean."

"No."

"You promise?"

I nod slowly. "We never could. It was forbidden."

"I know that. But maybe it doesn't have to be."

Sifu Phil isn't around to drill it into our heads anymore, so she's right. Maybe it doesn't have to be. Maybe the rules about sex were just something to keep us in line. Not some mystical rule of kung fu. I remember *Sifu* Phil's words, though: *There's a reason the monks are celibate. And it's not for fun.*

I don't say anything.

"Do you still want her?" she asks.

Yes.

Yes I do.

But Miranda doesn't want me. She wants Peter. The way she looks at him is how she used to look at me, before I stole her life away in some selfish quest to keep her safe. A decision I will regret forever. Not because it killed her feelings for me, but because of what it did to her.

Miranda still wrestles with the damage. I hear the words she sometimes mumbles in her sleep.

But she isn't standing in front of me right now. Someone else is. My heart feels black for even thinking this, but Sequel's the next best thing. And who knows? Maybe she's better.

"No," I say. "I don't want her."

Whatever it is about this place, Sequel is different. It's like she's alive for the first time. Her eyes are bright, not guarded. This isn't normal. It's just a building. It's just walls. There is nothing here. What does she want to keep secret?

"I want to trust you," she says.

"You can." I put my hands on her hips. "Hey, you can."

If the lie is on my face, I hide it the best I can. She can

trust me. That part wasn't a lie. But a sliver of my heart will always be with Miranda.

She steps away from me, and I guess we're leaving now. Good. My lips are still burning. But then she grips her T-shirt with both hands and pulls it over her head. I hear the fabric hit the floor. The light is dim, but I can make out her shape. My heart pounds so hard I think I might die right here. Suddenly my mouth is dry and tacky and I worry about kissing her like this.

"I can trust you," she says, halfway to a question.

I swallow, desire hammering me from all sides. I lick my lips. "Yes."

She kisses me again, softly like before, but then our lips press harder and our mouths open. She yanks my shirt over my head in one quick motion, but I don't lift my arms quick enough, so the sleeves rip. Guess how much I care. Her hands are cold on my blazing skin. The basement isn't so musty and dark and empty now. It's alive, like us. Her hands fumble with the button on my jeans, and—

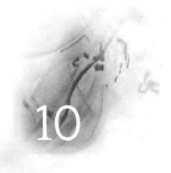

10

I push the band off hard enough to tear out some hair. It bounces off the roof, then the seat next to me, then up at the side window. Peter and Rhys spring upright in their seats. I look at the clock on the dashboard—2:02. Less than thirty minutes have passed, and Nina is now four hours ahead of us.

"I know where to go," I say.

They stare at me like I'm some kind of zoo animal.

"What happened?" Peter says.

"What did you see?" Rhys says.

"Just drive!" I close my eyes. "Just drive," I say again, quieter.

"I want a little more than that," Peter says. "Don't shut us out."

Rhys watches us, eyebrows raised. I'm so tired. Putting what I saw into words is the last thing I want to do.

But I tell them what I saw. All of it. My face is neutral; I can't let Peter know how it affected me. He'd be jealous, or wonder if there's something I'm leaving out. Or maybe he wouldn't. I've never seen him not confident before. But I don't want to chance it. I don't want to give him something else to think about, not when focus is so crucial.

"You said the room was empty, right?" Rhys says. "It already sounds like there's nothing there to find."

"It's called a clue," I say. "Maybe she went there. It felt like she was waiting for something, I don't know."

"She has a huge lead on us," Rhys says. "Guarantee if she went there she's moved on by now—well, I don't guarantee, but it's likely. We don't even know why she liked the place."

I sigh. "Maybe we can follow her trail. Rhys. You got a better idea?"

Peter cuts in. "Maybe her fixation on the place was some kind of leak from the latent personality. She didn't know why she was drawn to it, because she wasn't supposed to be yet. Not until the code changed her."

"Fine," Rhys says. "Say we get there and Nina is waiting for us. Then what?"

"We take her down," Peter replies. "We find out what the hell is going on."

I tell Peter to take the highway.

I can *taste* Sequel's kiss. This is wrong. I shouldn't have Noah's memories. They swim in my mind, waiting, an unlocked chest. I just have to pry open the lid. One thought and I'll know everything.

I wish I could go back. Actually, no I don't. I wouldn't have done anything differently. But that doesn't mean I like the outcome. I just have to remind myself the memories provided something to go on, even if it's as ambiguous as a dirty old building.

Peter gets off the highway and I tell him left or right or straight. The road reels past, overlaying with the memory of Noah's route. We pass the same gas station, the same broken street sign, until I say, "Here," and Peter stops the van. He parallel parks at the mouth of the alley. From this shallow angle I can see the wooden door Sequel kicked in. Someone wedged it back into the frame. The whole building appears abandoned. No signs say what it might have been. The street is even emptier than it was in Noah's memory—a scar from the dry run. Not many people stay in Cleveland anymore, if they can help it. The memory of the crazed people in the streets, literally insane with fear, is too fresh in the public mind.

"This is it," I say, pulling on my scaled gloves. The suit merges with the gloves, as seamless as everything else. Now I'm protected from toe to jaw.

"You're sure..." Rhys says. I don't bother to respond.

Peter goes over a simple plan. "If she's there we try to talk her down. If she isn't in the talking mood, we try to immobilize her. But if it's too dangerous, just use your judgment. Got it?"

"A fine plan," Rhys says, "if we can skip the talking part."

Peter pinches the bridge of his nose. "Rhys..."

"A fine plan," he repeats, this time seriously.

"Miranda?" Peter says.

"Got it. Nina was armed the last time I saw her." Like they didn't remember that detail.

Peter finishes with, "If she's not there, we look for something that says she was. Then we... I don't know. Figure something else out."

We gather our weapons and step into the chilled night. My stomach growls and my hands shake a little, probably not from low blood sugar. Stepping into the alley is strange, like putting on someone else's glasses. I see with my eyes *and* Noah's. He watches Sequel kick in the door, wondering what this place holds. Now I stand in front of the same door. In so many ways, I'm the same girl who kicked it in.

Peter's voice snaps me back to reality. "What do you see?"

Things I don't want to. "This is the door."

Rhys jogs to the front and tries to look through the windows, but they're too dirty and it's too dark. "Can't see a thing," he says. "Not sure how—"

Peter kicks in the door. I guess I'm not the only one out of patience.

The hinges were already broken, so the whole door screeches out of the frame and bounces down the steps into the basement. It slams flat and dust billows up from the sides, curling like smoke. I jump through the opening and onto the door, knowing immediately we're alone. I turn a slow circle, taking it in. The room feels ancient, like things happened here so long ago there's no one alive to remember them. The air smells only slightly better than the stench of the morgue.

Now that I'm here, I feel the draw of the place. We're supposed to be here, but I have no idea why. It's like an old memory brought back with a smell or a sound. Blurry, but familiar.

"Do you feel it?" I walk to the wall and lightly run my fingers over the bricks.

Behind me, Peter and Rhys have their eyes on me in a way that makes my skin crawl. I shouldn't have said what I did. If they're not feeling the draw, they're definitely hearing alarm bells.

"Something about this place," I say, trying to sound casual. "You don't feel it?" The back of my mind prickles where Noah's memories are. Maybe I'm imagining it.

"I don't," Peter says.

"I dunno," Rhys says.

Time has crumbled the mortar to ash, leaving the bricks crooked and unstable. I scrape at one with my fingernail. In fact, there's barely any mortar at all. Just chunks and flakes clinging to the old brick. White dust covers the floor near my feet, a few chips of brick strewn here and there. At the top of the wall is a black gap in the bricks, where one is jammed in sideways. Another one sticks out a few feet to my left. I don't need to recall Noah's memory to know the wall wasn't like this before. I lean closer and feel a draft on my cheeks through the tiny gaps in the bricks.

This wall was not whole just a short time ago. Someone rebuilt it.

I place both hands on brick that seems ready to crumble under my fingertips—

"There's nothing here," Rhys says.

—and push.

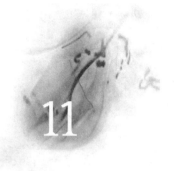

11

The wall collapses. Bricks rain down and clap against one another, powdering the mortar into a gray-white cloud. It took no effort at all. The wall simply fell over.

The room beyond stretches until it's less a room and more a tunnel. I visualize the building from the outside. It stood alone on this side of the street, next to empty weedy lots and the skeleton of a warehouse in the distance. Wherever this tunnel leads, it's not to another building, at least not one close by.

Nina came here and pushed through the wall, then put the bricks back together the best she could. At first I think, *Why bother to cover your tracks?* But then I realize that the only reason I gave the old wall a second look was because of Noah's memory. The rebuild wasn't perfect, but if we had tracked her here some other way, it's possible we wouldn't have noticed.

Peter kicks the opposite wall hard and bounces right off. I try the two adjacent walls—both solid.

I search Noah's memories for another time they were here. I skip the part where her mouth is on his neck, to the part where she stared at the wall but made no move to touch it. So the question is, what drew her when she was Sequel? It could be like Peter said—leakage from the Nina personality into the Sequel one. She knew this place was important, but didn't know why.

I guess it doesn't matter in the end. Except...I felt the same draw when we got here. Maybe my brain is just confused, trying to understand how I could remember this place even though it's my first time here.

Rhys stares down the tunnel. It's blacker than coal. He dusts his hands together and turns around. "Where do you think...?"

"Only one way to find out," Peter says.

Rhys makes a sound that's almost a laugh. "So Nina rebuilt the wall to hide her passing. Which means whatever she's doing is important enough to hide. I'm sure the wall took more than five minutes to rebuild."

Which means maybe her lead isn't so huge after all.

"Back to the *only one way to find out* part. I'll get the flashlights." Peter heads up the stairs to the alley, and before I can stop myself, I follow him outside.

I grab his wrist and pull him back. Who knows when we'll be alone again. My stomach grows heavy and sweat prickles under my suit. I don't want to look him in the eye and see what he's feeling, because I like pretending nothing bothers him. But Peter usually doesn't try to hide his feelings unless there's a tactical advantage. And that's exactly what I'm looking for—some sign to confirm I'm a member of the team, not a possible threat.

I get my answer right away, I think. His eyes are hard. Guarded.

"You still trust me?"

He swallows, which is all the answer I need. But I wait anyway.

"You want me to go?" I say.

"We talked about this. No."

I lower my voice so Rhys can't hear. "But you can't trust me until we know more," I say, like an accusation. I shouldn't say it that way, because it's not his fault.

"Are you asking me or telling me? What do you want me to do, Miranda? I'm sorry, I love you."

There it is, out in the open now. He can't unsay it. We've

been dancing around the phrase, both of us knowing it was too soon to say, both of us *wanting* to say it. Both of us too chicken.

Say it back.

"You do?" I say instead.

"Yeah." His face isn't expectant. He isn't waiting for anything in return. Or if he is, he's doing a great job of hiding it.

"So—" I begin, not even sure what I'm going to say. He grabs my arm and leads me away from the door.

"But I can't let that affect my judgment," he whispers. "I love you, and I trust you, but what if you...if you become *not* you, I have to be careful, you know." His eyes are wet.

You're supposed to feel different when someone tells you they love you. Right now I'd rather he shut me out completely. Not for the first time, I imagine taking off. Just stealing a car and driving anywhere. But I'd die before I let Nina get away with what she did. Plus, Peter could just find me with that stupid tracker I swallowed.

Peter reaches for me, but I lean away. "Don't, I might be dangerous."

"That's not fair. You said there was something about this place, and you asked me if I felt it. Tell me that doesn't sound weird."

He's right, of course.

"Just get the flashlights," I say, then head back for the basement.

Rhys is crouching, examining a brick, pretending he wasn't trying to eavesdrop. He lets it fall from his hands. "Everything okay?" he says with a kindness I don't usually hear in his voice. "Besides the obvious." He's smiling.

I almost smile back. "We'll see."

The tunnel is empty and black and shored up with wooden beams, like a mine. Someone built this. That idea burns away any thoughts I have for Peter and our relationship. *Someone built this.* More importantly, someone built this and Nina knew about it. Someone dug a hidden tunnel under the city, and then Nina showed up many years later, and I have no idea why, and neither do Peter and Rhys. It seems ancient, too old to be made by our creators. Cobwebs the size of quilts hang from the beams, which are so old they look like stone, not wood. Our three flashlight beams sway and cut through the black, showing more black. Our feet scrape lightly in the grit. Our breath is steady, our pace even. We don't talk because our bodies are live wires, listening for the smallest sounds, eyes peeled for whatever lies just beyond our beams. With every few steps I expect Nina to materialize out of the darkness, sword in hand.

We walk fifteen minutes over uneven ground. The air smells baked and old, like stones left in the sun.

Rhys is the first one to speak. "When do we give up and go back?"

Peter says, "You need to rest?"

"No, I'm just wondering who builds a damn tunnel behind a wall for no reason."

I step over a small boulder. "Who says there's no reason?"

He's quiet for twenty seconds. "I don't see one yet, is all."

And then we do. We come to railroad tracks. Two thin steel lines curve away into darkness. After another hundred feet, my beam catches the broad wooden back side of a four-wheeled cart. Like the kind I imagine coal miners used but bigger, big enough to hold all of us and then some. The huge wheels are rust-brown but solid. We circle the cart, shining our flashlights on it from every angle. The sides are made of old gnarled wooden planks banded together by thick iron strips.

"No engine," Rhys says.

"Would it have an engine?" Peter says.

Rhys leans over the side of the cart and shines his flashlight around. "No mechanism to propel us manually, so yeah, I'd expect an engine."

The cart looks old but whole. Not degraded in any way. I swing my legs over the side and plant my feet on metal rusted to the color of my hair.

And the cart begins to move.

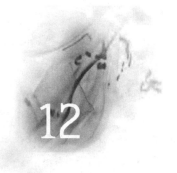

12

"**G**et out!" Peter says.

      "You get in!" I reply.

      No time for them to argue. Peter and Rhys sprint after me—I'm accelerating quicker than I expected—and I pull them up and over the back end.

      Within seconds we're traveling too fast to jump off. The wind buffets us and we sit down, heads just above the sides of the cart, barreling into darkness. The wheels howl and screech on the track, vibrating the cart's frame, making my teeth buzz. The ground is still flat; the cart is definitely moving under its own power.

      "We didn't think this one through," Peter shouts.

"Did you want to walk the rest of the way?" I shout back, hoping this was the right decision. I try to relax the tension in my muscles, but with only darkness ahead it feels like we could drop off the rails and into an underground cavern at any second.

Rhys says, "If Nina made this trip, we're in the right place. Soon we'll find out why. Or maybe the cart will come off the rails and dash our heads against the walls." He laughs, but we don't. His face grows serious as he aims the flashlight under his chin. *Supposed to laugh in times like these,* he says, too quiet for us to hear over the noise, but I read his lips.

The cart screams, the wind tears at my hair. Portions of the tunnel are lighted now. I see them in the distance as glowing yellow specks, and the next second we're there, and the next they're behind us, dwindling to darkness. I can't even guess how fast we move. For a while I kneel at the front, hands gripping the front wall, staring forward into the black. The wail of metal on metal knocks any thoughts out of my head before they can fully form.

I lean back against the cart and settle down. It's almost comfortable, minus the hair lashing my eyes. To my left, Peter strobes with light every ten seconds. His face is hard and determined, watching the way ahead of us.

The cart vibrates under me, rocking. A hundred miles an

hour, at least. More. And it doesn't end. We don't drop off into a cavern, and I stop expecting us to. We're going somewhere, that much is clear.

I stay awake for what feels like an hour, but nothing changes. We keep flying on the rails, but the route has become smooth. No curves to press us into the walls of the cart. Just a steady hum, a subtle tremor I feel with my entire body. The cart is doing its best to lull me to sleep.

Peter touches my arm lightly, startling me. "Rest," he says. "I'll let you know if something changes."

I nod, grateful, because I don't know when I'll get to close my eyes again. Somehow I drift into something half aware and half asleep.

I'm outside a log cabin nestled against the sheer face of a cliff. I remember this place. We were doing a training exercise in the national park and came across this cabin. Noah convinced me to go inside because we were both stiff with the freezing winds. Inside there was a fire going, but no one around. We shared our first kiss next to the flames, one side of my face baking in the heat, the other stinging with the chill. I was fifteen.

Now the trees around me are green and alive with bird-song. I walk to the cabin and push through the door. Across the room, an unnecessary fire roars in the hearth. A knotty wood table sits in the middle with two cups on it. I can see from here the cups are filled with cocoa and mini marshmallows. Noah sits at the table, smiling. I sit down across from him, smiling back. I warm my hands on my mug, and he takes a sip.

"Let me out," he says. "Let me help you. I promise I can."

I want him to help. "Okay," I say.

"It might hurt. There isn't much room in here."

"I'm ready," I say.

He licks his lips and takes another sip. I raise my own mug and tilt some of the cocoa into my mouth. It's the most delicious thing I've ever tasted. Then it's not—it's a thousand degrees and my insides bake and turn to ash and I open my mouth to scream—

I wake up to Peter's lips against my ear.

No, it's Rhys.

"Wake up, we're slowing."

I move to the front of the cart as the dream disperses. I try to catch it, but it'd be easier to catch smoke. The cart is no longer moving under its own power; it coasts. The tunnel is lit more frequently now, equal pools of black and light.

"How long was I out?"

"I don't know," Rhys says. "I lost track of time."

The pitch of the screeching wheels drops as we slow, as does the wind in my ears. Peter is awake, in the same position I last saw him.

"Really, how long?" I say.

Rhys shrugs. "No idea. Definitely hours."

I can't believe it; the news stuns me enough that I have to just sit here and think about the magnitude of the tunnel. Where are we? We could be anywhere. The amount of work to build this place . . . It had to take forever to hew the tunnel from rock, to install the lights and beams. All so something could travel underground—but for what purpose, I have no idea. Nina might not have come this way at all, but the length of the trip makes me feel confident we're on the right path. After all, the magical cart just waiting for us couldn't have been a coincidence. The amount of unknowns makes me want to turn around, but it's obviously too late for that. My skin prickles with the feeling that whatever lies ahead is big. If only because the tunnel should be impossible. And all the while my heart rate climbs as I anticipate/dread what comes next. Nina might be right around the corner.

It takes another full minute to slow enough for the wheels to quiet. A bright light shines down the tunnel, the size of a penny held at arm's length. Peter tenses beside me. I fight the same reaction and try to stay loose.

The cart rolls to a final stop.

I jump off the front of the cart, pull Beacon off my back, and use my left hand to snatch the revolver from my thigh. I hear the boys hop down, several muted metallic scrapes as they pull their weapons too.

Behind me, the wheels groan against the track.

I spin around to see the cart reversing. Like it was programmed to return the second it delivered us.

Rhys takes a few running steps after it, then skids to a stop, shaking his head.

"That's not good," he says.

They look at me like I knew it was going to happen.

"Not my fault," I say, though it kind of is, since I got into the cart first.

"We keep moving," Peter says.

"Well, we can't exactly go back," Rhys replies. "I don't like it."

"Me neither," Peter says.

I let my weapons dangle at my sides. "We're close. Rhys is right, there's nowhere else to go."

We stand there for a moment, in the near-dark and silence. I think we're waiting for one of us to come up with a better idea. Finally I turn away and walk deeper into the tunnel, toward the bright light.

"Technically, we *could* go back," Rhys calls after me. Then he mutters, "There's nothing good about this place." Almost like a plea. Rhys is unnerved, which unnerves me. If Noah were here, he'd call Rhys something derogatory, even though he'd be feeling the same sense of wrongness we all do. Call it our training keeping us on edge, but I know it's just regular old human fear, the darker kind that comes when you don't understand.

Two seconds later, their footsteps start after me.

We walk for ten minutes, and the light gets brighter and brighter.

"Be ready," Rhys whispers beside me. I hear Peter pull the hammer back on his revolver.

We spread out over the last fifty feet, then leave the tunnel behind for a huge underground chamber.

Huge doesn't begin to describe it. Think stadium-size, complete with an enormous dome roof you can't see with just one glance. Lights dot the ceiling in a grid pattern too bright to look at. Tunnels like the one we came through are built around the circumference, right into the rock, like the tunnels people use to get to their seats in a stadium. Only triple the amount. At first glance, there seems to be a hundred, some of them stacked three high, a grid of openings that now remind me less of stadium tunnels and more of drawers in a morgue.

Each tunnel has a label that sends a chill from the base of my spine to the top of my head. They say things like CHICAGO and LOS ANGELES and AUSTIN and TAMPA and MIAMI and BUFFALO and CHEYENNE and SEATTLE.

Cities. All the cities in America I could name, and some I couldn't, like TWIN FALLS.

None of this is the weird part.

In the center of the cavern is a flat black circle the size of a small lake. I walk toward it slowly. The black surface reflects no light, so I can't tell what it is. It seems to be *something*, not a hole in the ground. But not liquid, either. Just . . . *black*.

I step closer.

"Let me go first," Peter says behind me.

My mind shows me Noah charging into the darkness of the lab. I am done letting anyone else go first. "No, wait."

My eyes go to the tunnels again. So many paths, all stemming from this central hub like spokes on a wheel. I slide Beacon onto my back, feel the click as it adheres to my armor, but keep the silver revolver in my grasp.

"Anyone have a good feeling about this?" Rhys says.

It's so quiet I can hear the blood in my ears. I can't take my eyes off the lake. I am staring into the abyss, literally. Instinct is screaming at me to run, but I press on. Noah would have, and I'm sure Nina did.

I approach the lake slowly, waiting for a change or a ripple, a reflection, but it doesn't alter. Soon I'm kneeling at the edge. My eyes begin to ache, but I don't look away.

"What are you doing?" Peter says. He grabs my arm, but I reach forward with the other one and touch the black.

Nothing happens. My hand disappears to the wrist, but I feel nothing, literally nothing, like my hand has been disconnected. The black isn't a liquid; it's not anything. I pull my hand out and feeling returns as I do, first my wrist, then palm, then fingers, then fingertips.

"Not a dead end," Rhys says. He's staring into the lake with unfocused eyes, like it has him caught in a trance.

"Might as well be," Peter says. "It's not like we're going to jump in." He pulls me up and I let him, thinking, *We're probably going to jump in, and you know that. We came all this way.* He grabs my hand and inspects it—the armor is fine. The smaller scales on my fingers are intact and flawless.

Rhys kneels for a closer look. "We can't make it back on foot. No food or water."

"Are there any carts in the tunnels?" Peter says, casting his gaze over the floor-level openings. Some of the tunnel entrances are lit and smooth and feel finished, while some are shadowed and craggy, like open mouths waiting to chew us up.

"It would take hours to search each one," I say, flexing my hand. It felt odd in the black, but not wrong. Just . . . missing. "This is our path. Nina came here, I know it."

"You can't be sure," Rhys says.

"Nina was supposed to gather something called the eyeless," I go on, ignoring him. "Sequel told me. If Nina came here, I don't see where else she could go."

"Down one of the tunnels, maybe," Peter says. "You don't know."

"You'll be able to track me," I say, tapping the small pack lashed to my waist.

"Track you when you fall to your death? We don't know what's down there."

"I'm going to jump in," I say.

He's eyeing me now, and I can guess why. "Do you really want to, or is something else telling you to do that?"

Rhys squints at Peter, not sure exactly what he means—but I know. "Wait," Rhys says, pointing at the ground. "There." I follow his finger six feet to the left, to a collection of small footprints in the light dust. The scaled bottoms of Nina's feet are clear. She was here, at this very spot.

"What do you think now?" I ask Peter.

"That she definitely came here. But is that proof she jumped in? Not exactly. And answer my question. Why do you want to jump so badly?"

"I don't, but why would all these tunnels connect to here?" I admit my desire to go through might seem a bit suspicious, but I believe it's the right direction, and I think deep down he does too.

All I know for certain is that the lake is something we don't understand. It's not natural. And I prefer my enemies of the flesh and blood variety.

"Are you really willing to do this?" Rhys says. "I am if you are."

I nod. "It's that or we take a chance down a tunnel. We're wasting time." I turn to Peter. "Make a decision. Please."

Peter shakes his head. "I don't know. None of this seems real."

So I settle it. I do what Noah did for me.

I bend my knees and leap into the black.

13

I wake up in a room.

I'm on my back, heart thrumming. Above me, a single yellow bulb is so dim the filaments are visible. My stomach churns. I roll onto my hands and knees, open my mouth. Fire rushes up my throat and spews from my lips into a black puddle between my hands. The black stuff coming out of my mouth terrifies me. I'm dying. If you're puking black sludge, you're dying.

I'm surrounded by three walls of rough gray rock and one wall of vertical iron bars. The bars are orange and brown with surface rust.

Not a room, a cell.

Somehow my suit is gone, gloves too. The floor tilts under

me, and I close my eyes to wait for the sensation to pass, but it doesn't.

I remember everything before my leap of faith, which means someone *stole* my armor and dressed me in these ragged cloth garments that barely cover my legs and chest. The shirt is sleeveless, with a tight collar around my throat. Basically a burlap bag with a hole cut for my head. The shorts are rough scratchy fibers poorly sewn together. The thought of someone undressing and dressing me while I was unconscious sends a violent shiver across my shoulders.

I remember leaping over the emptiness. Peter's cry and Rhys's gasp. Then nothingness. It was only a second ago.

I spit leftover black goop from my mouth, run my tongue over my teeth. The rock floor is so cold it's sucking my body heat. I sit on my butt to keep as little skin contact as possible. Behind me, something bounces off the floor. I spin around, rising to my feet with my hands up, ready to tear its eyes out. It was just a pebble that came loose from the wall. It rolls toward a wooden bucket in the corner that is just outside the reach of the feeble light. I let out a miserable half-crying sound and squeeze my eyes shut, nearly falling back on my butt. A single tear escapes onto my cheek.

Under the ball of my right foot is a crease, a line that bisects the floor of the cell. I feel a vibration through it. I go down on my hands and knees again, next to the sludge that I threw up, and put my ear to the cold, smooth rock. I hear a rushing noise ...liquid. Water gurgling under the floor, maybe.

I've always wondered if my experiences made me better prepared for anything. I liked to think I was more capable than your average girl, and not just physically. But I don't think I am. I'm two seconds away from tucking myself into a ball and crying myself back to sleep. Seconds ago I was jumping into the lake, and now I'm here, dressed in different clothing, a prisoner for the second time in less than twelve hours.

I crawl to the bucket. It's filled with water. The wooden lip is too thick to drink from, so I cup some of the water in my palm and lift it to my mouth. It's cool and clear, exactly how water should be. I slurp a few more handfuls until the foul taste in my mouth weakens. The drink calms me a little, which isn't the best thing, because then I can think. Jumping against Peter's wishes has made me a captive of...well, who really knows. My money is on the creators.

If Peter and Rhys followed me, they probably share the same fate. My fault. I had to jump in like some kind of don't-give-a-shit badass.

I want to go to the bars and call out to them, in the hopes that they're stuck in a nearby cell, but I'm afraid. Afraid Peter and Rhys won't answer. Afraid they will.

But I say something out loud anyway, just to hear my own voice. "I'm all alone."

"No you're not," a voice says behind me.

I whirl around, hands balled into fists.

Noah stands in the opposite corner of my cell.

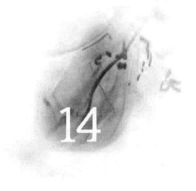

14

I'm dead.

Some of the confusion drains away, leaving me empty but less afraid. I may be dead, but you can't hurt the dead.

"You're not dead," Noah says. "At least, I'm pretty sure you're not. Yeah, no. You're not. I'd know." His eyes glitter black, little shards of onyx. They fit right in with this place. The black scales of his suit hide where his wound should be. However he got here, we obviously didn't come the same way.

That leaves one other possibility.

He seems to know what I'm going to ask before I ask it. "I'm not a different version of me, either," he says. "Remember the peanut butter?"

"Yes. So where am I?"

He shrugs. He wears his armor, but no weapons.

"No clue," he says. "Not anywhere I'd like to hang out, but who would?"

I laugh. It bursts from my mouth painfully and echoes off the cramped stone walls. "Then what are you doing here?"

"This is going to sound crazy," he says with a smile, and I laugh again. I can't believe it's him. He looks so real. His smile, the dimple that sometimes appears in his right cheek. Tears are streaming down my face.

"Try me," I say.

"Everything is fuzzy right now." He crinkles his nose. "But there's something I'm supposed to remember, something I didn't know before, but I do now. That sounds crazy."

"Kind of."

I step closer, entering the haze of light, and so does he. The light casts V-shaped shadows under his eyes. I reach out, slowly, and touch his neck with my fingertips. I peel the black scales off his neck.

And feel his flesh underneath.

His unmarred flesh. Whole. Uncut.

And impossible.

"This isn't real." I close my eyes.

When he speaks, his breath touches my cheeks. "It's real in your mind. I feel you the same way. I can't explain it."

"Can you hear my thoughts?"

He shakes his head. "Only when you want me to. Can you hear mine?"

I shake my head back. The secret of my short past is safe.

He puts a finger under my chin and tilts it up. Rubs his thumb across my lower lip. I taste the salt of my tears. I can see him, feel him, smell him. My knees shake.

"But you died," I whisper.

"In a way," he replies, then leans forward and presses his lips against mine.

The lightbulb flickers, buzzing. My eyes snap open and my hands are raised in front of me, curled, as if I was hugging someone and now they're gone.

Noah's gone.

"Where are you?" I whisper, not expecting an answer.

"Here."

Noah's voice. In my head, but like he's talking right next to me.

I can only manage one thought—*How?*

"I don't know."

"Come back. Let me see you." I don't want to be alone. I feel his phantom kiss on my lips still. I don't know why I kissed him back. It felt terribly wrong and terribly right at the same time.

"If my voice in your head is a little strange, guess how it feels for me."

I spin around. Noah is leaning with both shoulders against the wall, arms folded. A cocky, careless pose. So Noah.

"And you're not really here...."

"I thought that part was obvious by now," he says. He's pretending like we didn't just kiss, which is fine with me.

"Are you okay?" Such a stupid question. I regret it even as my lips form the words.

He blinks rapidly. "Not really. But I'm managing. You know I always do. Something hurts, though." He taps his head with the heel of his hand. "I'm supposed to be doing something."

"What?"

"I don't know. Give me more than thirty seconds."

It really is him.

"So where the hell are we?"

"It looks like a prison cell." He smiles. He doesn't smirk.

For a second I think everything might be okay. If this isn't a dream, or hell, and Noah really is here ... well, I'm not alone. Even if he's just in my head.

"It's you. Really," I say, unable to keep the tears out of my voice.

He nods grimly, frowning. In life, he only frowned when he was trying to show he was telling the truth. He pats himself on the chest and legs, making sure he's all there. "Is this how you remember me?"

A chill covers me when I realize that being imprisoned holds a greater danger than boredom—my memory shots are out of reach. I'll be okay for a while, but I can't expect to be going home anytime soon. Even if I manage to survive in here a day or two, it'll all be for nothing if I can't keep my memories. Soon I'll be clueless, confused, without an identity.

"I don't have any shots," I say, mostly to myself. "You don't happen to have any, do you?" It's a half joke.

Noah pats where his pockets would be if he had any. "Fresh out. But don't worry about that yet. Worry about—"

The floor begins to vibrate through the bottoms of my freezing feet. A mechanical buzz that almost tickles. More pebbles tumble down the walls.

And the floor begins to split apart at the seam.

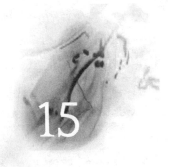

15

Slowly, the two sides of the floor retract into the walls. In the middle, a black gulf grows wider, and I see that I was right—there is water under the floor. Black water. As black as the lake I jumped through, but broken with vibrations from the moving floor. It reflects the yellow light of the bulb above.

"Move!" Noah shouts.

My feet are on either side, slowly pulling me into a split. I push off with my right foot and step onto Noah's half. It takes me that long to realize that, yeah, the cell is about to dump me into the black water. And there's nothing I can do to stop it.

"Do something!" Noah says, grabbing my shoulder.

It's not just me in here; it's Noah. I lunge for the bars and try to stick my feet through them, but the floor outside the cell is covered in tiny spikes I don't see until they cut me. Hot blood slicks the balls of my feet.

The gulf takes up a third of the floor now; I won't have a place to stand much longer.

"Do something, Mir."

I stop being a slow idiot and plant my foot on the remaining meter of floor, then kick the door where it's most discolored at the hinges. My foot leaves a smear of blood on the rusted bars. Hot pain lances up to my knee, which happens when you kick solid iron. I kick twice more, leaving thicker smears, blood oozing freely from my cut foot.

"C'mon, Miranda! Kick!" Noah stands off to the side. He claps his hands. "DO IT!"

I kick again and again, until the door is out of reach and my toes are numb. My foot aches, the cut burns. The bars thrum in their frame. I grab the bars to gain a little more reach, then awkwardly kick the door a final time. The wrong part of my foot connects; my ankle twists painfully and I cry out.

"Again!"

"I *can't.*"

"Shut up. *Again.*"

I scream and leap onto the door as my footing disappears,

grabbing both bars and planting my feet vertically to either side. I pull with everything in me, arms shaking, shoulders burning, back aching as I hover over the water.

"Don't you dare give up!" Noah says.

My legs are throbbing hot and red, and my head is about to burst. The hinges groan like the rest of me, but do not budge. My whole body is on fire.

I'm holding on to the cage like a monkey. My arms shake, yet I hold fast. The floor is gone now, the black water waiting to swallow me whole. I cling to the cage with my knees, not wanting to put my throbbing feet back on the spikes. I tremble from top to bottom, and the door rattles quietly in its frame. If I could only rest for a moment, take a deep breath, I could hold on longer.

I crane my head around, but Noah is gone.

"Don't leave me alone," I say aloud.

I stay alone.

He's not ignoring me; I don't feel him anywhere.

The thought of losing him again makes my brain fuzz gray, refusing to even imagine the possibility. I groan and knock my head against the bars, like it'll shake him loose.

"I'm here," he says in my head.

"Where did you go?" A terrible realization sets in—I won't be able to hold on forever. Even now my fingers are numb from holding most of my weight. There's a steady *drip drip drip* as blood from my foot drops into the water.

"I don't know. I can't control it. It's like your mind is trying to push me out. I can only show up when you're calm."

"I'm calm!" I scream, as the muscles in my arms cramp into rocks.

"I don't belong here. Not enough room—"

He cuts out.

"Noah?"

Then the bolts holding the top of the cell door burst down like tiny bullets, pinging off my shoulders and shooting into the water. I feel tension release in the door and only have time for a breath before the whole thing falls inward and dumps me into the water.

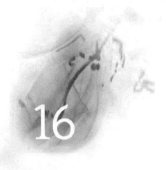

16

The door wasn't made to float. I grasp the bars and try to wrestle it out of the way, but it just pushes me down. The black water lets in no light and stings my eyes. I squeeze them shut, grabbing for the next bar over to pull myself around the door. I'm not going to make it; I'm sinking too fast. The pressure in my ears builds, builds, then aches, then throbs.

Next the bars are ripped from my hands and a current slams me full in the back, thrusting me forward.

The warm water gurgles in my ears, stings the wounds on my feet. Seconds pass as I tumble once, twice, no sense of direction now. A column of water pistons me from the side, and I spin again, laterally. I open my eyes and toss my head around and see nothing. No surface. I'm not going to be able to find up. I don't know which way to kick. My eyes burn; my mouth burns. The black water tastes like stomach acid. Pretty soon my mouth is going to open and I'm going to suck the liquid into my lungs. Maybe it won't be so bad.

Noah, I call out desperately. *Don't leave me alone.*

He doesn't answer. Maybe he was never really there to begin with.

I sink deeper as the current relents. Sinking means the surface must be the other way. I try kicking that way and feel something tug on my ankle. I kick out, but it's already gone. Then another current hauls me sideways. This isn't a natural current—I'm getting hammered from all sides, pushed and pulled around. I have to open my mouth now. Noah isn't here to share his breath. I'm alone. If he hadn't kissed me that one time, kept me alive, I wouldn't have lived to kill him. I wouldn't have lived to die here alone in the dark.

The water pushes me farther, and suddenly another wall of water slams into me from the bottom, pushing me straight up. My lungs are about to burst. This is it—I open my mouth to scream and bubbles surge over my face, and then I break the surface, heaving, sucking in water droplets and coughing.

Two sets of rough hands haul me out of the water and throw me on my back. I try to open my eyes, but it burns too much.

A moment passes where I consider fighting, just lashing out and releasing all the psychic energy I can muster, but that wouldn't be smart. I'm half-blind and weak in an unknown location with unknown enemies. And I'm not dead yet, so that counts for something.

"Noah . . ." I say, as the filthy water pools around me.

"What did you say?"

I crack my eyes against the sting. A man looms over me. He has bristly black hair in a military cut, dark olive skin, and eyes as black as the water. He could be thirty or forty. His clothing is paramilitary—black combat pants tucked into big black boots, and a thick black vest with many pockets and zippers. The guy likes black. And fingerless gloves, apparently.

The man nudges me with his toe. "I asked what you said."

We're inside a building unlike any I've seen before. It's shaped like a hollow beehive, with the lowest levels having the largest circumference. The inside circumference of each level looks down over the open center of the structure. In the very middle, close to me, a redwood-size column rises from the bottom floor to the top. Catwalks branch off the column, like it's the trunk of some metallic Christmas tree.

Next to me is the hatch they must've pulled me through. I can hear the water gurgling beneath it.

"Maybe she doesn't speak English, sir," a girl's voice says behind me.

The man crouches. "I think she does," he says. "Did you hear me?"

"I heard you," I reply. They haven't impressed me enough to warrant an immediate answer. I'm soaked and sore and pissed off. And confused—they don't recognize me. If this is a creator-run facility, why did they wonder if I spoke English?

"See?" the man says.

"Is there a reason I'm wet?"

"Protocol," the man says. "You are in a weakened state. The water has a temporary property that slows reaction time, effectively tranquilizing you."

No kidding; I feel wiped out, even though I've caught my breath.

"Great," I say. "Did anyone else . . . show up?" Tranquilized or not, I can still feel. Mostly anger. These people have touched me against my will, and I am not free. Until that changes, the anger will burn inside me. I'll wear it like the armor these people stole from me.

The man says nothing, just studies me with hard eyes. It's like he's surprised.

"Where am I? Where are my friends?"

"How did you come through the gate?" he says.

"I'll answer your question after you answer mine."

He kicks me in the ribs so hard, my lungs seize. Stabbing pain rolls through my chest in time with my pulse. I almost let loose with my power. The pressure builds in my head, but I stop at the last second and roll onto my hands and knees. If I send out fear-waves, I'll just need a memory shot sooner rather than later. Plus, I don't want these people to know what I can do until I'm ready to do it.

"Where are the others I came through with?" I say, once my breath returns. I'll just keep asking, I don't care. I see the girl and another man now, wearing the same outfit as the first man, but theirs are a dusky red, like dried blood or rose petals. They wear red cloth masks over their noses and mouths, in the shape of an upside-down triangle, like bandits. The man has shoulder-length blond hair, and the girl's hair is short and black, like Nina's. Her skin is dark, and the man's is so pale it's like he's never seen the sun. All three of them just watch me, motionless and emotionless.

"Where are they?" I have to fight to get the words out; my ribs are throbbing. I struggle into a kneeling position, putting my back to the two in red since they're clearly not in charge.

"Alive," the man in black finally answers.

I nearly sag to the floor as relief weakens my limbs. *Alive.* I just have to cling to that—*alive.*

My rags stick to me, showing the outline of my body. I want to cover myself, but the three don't leer at me. They study me like I'm some kind of alien. Not a person—a thing.

The man crouches before me and uses his thumb and

forefinger to turn my face left and right, as if inspecting me. I meet his gaze steadily.

Then he says, "You look just like the girl who came through a few hours ago. Do you know her?"

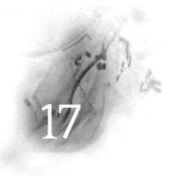

17

I stand up.

Too fast, I guess. The man in black rises with me, and the two in red kick the backs of my knees to make me fall forward. I brace for another strike that doesn't come. Black water drips off me. My hair hangs heavily, and the subtle acidic smell of it makes my empty stomach twist. I fight the scream of pure frustration rising in my chest.

"Patience," I hear Noah say.

It startles me. *Are you here?*

Two seconds pass and he doesn't reply, and my spirits sag further.

Slowly, I raise my head to look up at the man in black. He seems content to just stare at me for the next hour. "Where is this girl?" I say, voice hard as ice. *Why don't you know who she is?* I don't ask.

He ignores me completely. To the two in red, he says, "Send the other girl to the lower block." Their footsteps travel away, brisk and solid. "No contact," he adds before they're out of earshot.

We're alone now, and he doesn't seem worried at all. No hint of nervousness in his eyes or posture. For all I know, he could take me in a fight. And if he sees what I'm capable of, he may get extra cautious and make it harder to escape later. Not to mention I would die rather than leave Rhys and Peter behind.

Maybe I can appeal to this guy logically.

"I think there's been a misunderstanding," I say. It's possible he's not affiliated with the creators—which would be great —but that leaves the tunnel and black lake unexplained, since Nina clearly knew about them. And she's clearly one of the creators' weapons. Or Mrs. North's, at least.

"Of what nature?" he says.

Slowly I stand up again, making sure my hands are visible. I speak calmly. "I don't know where I am or how I got here. And whatever you think you know about the other girl, know that she's already killed one of my friends. She'll kill you too, if you get in her way."

The man in black studies me for a moment longer, then

turns away. Thirty seconds pass. I try to think of a plan, but my brain is white noise. Soon I hear the two in red returning from a corridor off the main floor. I make note of four corridor openings, one each to my north, south, east, and west.

"She's ready, Commander," the girl says.

"What are you the commander of?" I say, before I think too much about it. It's a fair question.

"Don't speak—" the red man begins.

The commander silences him with a raised hand. "Leave," he says. Their footsteps recede again, no questions or hesitation.

"My name is Gane," he says. "I am commander of the Verge, and steward of what remains of this city."

"Miranda North," I say. "At your service."

Gane's mouth is open, like he can't believe I'm capable of sarcasm.

Then he laughs and says, "Walk with me." He heads in the direction the two in red went. Now that he's moving, his liquid grace is obvious; he glides like a ghost, boots barely making a sound. "I said walk." He doesn't bother to look back.

I'm not interested in making him come back for me. I walk.

"If I ask you something important, will you listen to me?" I say.

I'm a few steps behind Commander Gane. He doesn't mind showing his back to me. There's some weird bump under his vest between his shoulder blades. I visualize myself stepping forward and driving a fist into his spine. And then what? I need to pick his brain, but passing up the chance to attack him and escape makes my skin crawl with lost opportunities.

"Ask me," he says.

"We came through wearing black suits, like armor. Where are they?"

He keeps walking. "Why?"

"We need something hidden in the suits. If we don't get it, we'll lose our memories. Me and the others." Reminding myself of what I would lose won't help right now, yet I keep doing it.

He leads me into the corridor, which is really a circular tunnel hewn from rock. The walls are smooth and lined with torches. The kind made of wood with one end on fire. They flicker and paint our dancing shadows across the walls. It's like we passed from the future into medieval times.

"We'd lose *all* of them," I continue. "Please. We'd be no use to you then."

He finally glances back passively. "Who said I want to use you?"

I try to think of a reply, but all I can come up with is *What do you want?* I won't ask him because I doubt he'd give a real answer, and I won't give him the power to ignore me. I remember the single word Noah uttered in my mind.

Patience.

The tunnel curves left and stops at a black iron door. Gane pushes through it, revealing a room with two cells at the far end, with the same iron bars and seams in the floor.

The right cell holds Peter and Rhys.

The left one holds Nina.

18

The relief at seeing them outweighs everything else, infusing me with new energy. I run toward the bars with their names on my lips. The door slams shut behind me.

Nina stands in her cage to the left, watching us with her arms folded behind her back. Everything I felt when Noah died comes rushing back, souring my stomach. She's lucky those bars are between us. I try to ignore her because I don't want her face spoiling what it's like to see Peter and Rhys again. All three of them wear the same rough shorts and sleeveless cloth shirts.

My hands slip through the bars and grasp Peter's. Rhys

grabs my forearm, and we hold one another. Our breath is heavy, like we just ran a mile. We're together, touching, solid and whole and alive. If I can keep it that way, nothing else matters.

"You're both safe," I say at last. Peter ducks his head forward, and I press my face to the bars and our lips touch lightly.

That's enough to bring Noah back. I feel him standing behind me, like a sixth person suddenly entered the room. I break Peter's kiss too early and turn around.

"You remember how you kissed me in your cell? You kissed me like we used to kiss. The very same way."

Noah ...

What he says is true, and it makes me want to cry. I shouldn't have done that.

He ignores me, staring languidly into Nina's cell. But that can't be right—how can he see her? Is this just how my brain is visualizing him?

Gane asks me, "Which would you like to stay in?"

Fear flickers in Nina's eyes, then disappears behind a stoic mask. A mask I would believe if she hadn't taken a step back. Some primal urge rises in me at her show of weakness. I want to tear the bars apart and share her cell for a minute or two.

"Don't put her in here with me," she says. "She'll kill me."

"Why would she kill you?" Gane says.

"To keep me from sharing information."

"Really. Information of what nature?"

"Of the nature you want. The kind you've been searching for."

Gane raises an eyebrow. "I'll need more than that."

"Commander Gane, I was sent here to take the eyeless from your lands. I know where the Torch is." She points at me. "She doesn't. Therefore I am useful. She isn't. She doesn't even know what I'm talking about. Look at her."

"Miranda," Noah says, his voice cutting through me like a sword. He's right in front of me now. "I remember something."

In my mind, Noah shows me the monsters we've feared. The ones who will "conquer the world." The images are blurry, corrupted somehow, but I see enough. They're spindly and milk-white, hunched on all fours even though they're human-oid. They move like wolves. I see them flowing through the ruins of a city, galloping on claw-tipped hands and feet. Something controls them. It's a slender shaft with a red orb on one end, glowing brilliantly, like a bloody star.

The images snap out of focus, and I'm back in the room.

"Did you see?" Noah says. "Did you see? How did I know that?"

I don't know, I think.

"There's more, I know there is." Noah paces away, hands laced on top of his head. "Give me a minute."

When I turn back, everyone is still staring at Nina.

Gane's stone face veils his curiosity, but not completely. "You told me that before," he says to her. "Make me believe you."

Nina steps to the bars and grabs them with both hands. "I know how to control them. I can prove it to you. I'll lead them through the Black."

Through the Black . . .

Her voice is steady. "I know where the Torch is."

I try to fit the pieces together—the Torch, the Black, and the eyeless. *Through the Black,* she said. I went through the Black. And now I'm here.

What's the Black?

"I don't know yet," Noah says. "Some kind of transport system. I can't see it. Dammit!" He spins and punches Gane in the face, but his fist passes through like a ghost, as we both knew it would. He walks away with his hands clasped behind his head, breathing through clenched teeth, frustration that he can't do *anything* written all over his body.

Gane remains quiet.

"Ask yourself this," Nina says, not giving up. "How could I know about the Torch?"

Good question. A better question is *How do I know about the*

Torch? Noah somehow granted me the understanding that the Torch is an instrument to control the eyeless, but how did *he* know?

"There are thousands of eyeless," Gane says. "Tens of thousands. The Torch is a myth. And you are an interloper. Anything that comes through the Black is not to be trusted, not ever."

Nina shakes her head behind the bars, gripping them tightly. "Don't be a fool."

Rhys says to Gane, "Hey, Cobra Commander, maybe you should listen to us instead."

Gane holds up a hand. "Quiet."

As if by the motion of his hand, the bars between the two cells rise into the ceiling, rumbling and scraping, iron on stone. Now Nina shares the same space as Peter and Rhys. She steps back again. Smart girl.

"You will be together while I think on this," Gane says. "I'm going to open the cell door. Make no move toward it, or I will strike you down." To my right, a door cut into the bars swings open.

Now there's unbroken space between Commander Gane and Peter and Rhys. They're smart enough to believe Gane, so they stay put. I don't. I stride forward and Peter wraps his arms around me and lifts my feet off the ground. He sets me down and kisses below my ear and whispers, "Where are we?"

I have no answer for him.

The cell door closes behind me, followed by the bang of the big iron door opening and closing.

Alpha team is alone again. The three of us are on one side of the cell, Noah and Nina on the other.

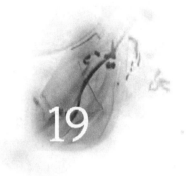

19

Noah walks a circle around Nina slowly, less than a foot away. Fresh tears fall from his chin. "You killed me," he whispers. "You killed me. You killed me." I keep waiting for Nina to notice him, but she doesn't. He's just some kind of illusion, an expression in my mind. I guess I have to keep reminding myself of that.

"What do we do with her?" Rhys says.

"We don't do anything," Peter says.

I blink, and Noah disappears. This time it felt like he'd seen enough and decided to leave on his own. Not sure if that's a good sign or not. I should tell the others he's still here. Alive and not alive.

"Remind them about the memory shots," Noah says in my head.

"We need our shots," I say.

Nina watches us from just twenty feet away, hands loose at her sides. She rolls her head from shoulder to shoulder; her neck cracks. It would take no time to cover the distance, to drive my fists into her body until she begged for forgiveness. I could make her tell Noah she's sorry, so sorry, that she knows he had so much longer to live, that he missed out on his whole life, all the good parts we had dreamed about as a team, when the fighting would be over for good.

My hands shake.

"I don't want to fight," she says.

"Well, of course not," Rhys says. I touch his arm, hearing the anger in his voice. "There are three of us, one of you."

"Why are you here?" I ask her.

Her eyes flit between us, assessing us, identifying weak points. I know, because I'm doing the same thing to her.

"Exactly what I told Commander Gane," she replies.

"That means nothing to me."

"Sequel," Peter says softly as he steps up beside me. "I know you're in there."

Nina spits on the floor. "Please. Save it."

Rhys steps forward, and this time I don't touch his arm.

Nina walks backward until she hits the wall, then slides down to her butt. She licks her lips. "Just stay on your side. You may be able to kill me, but not before I kill one of you."

"She's right," Noah says. "Just leave her alone."

Quiet. His voice is like a cracked whip in my mind, shattering my focus.

"You think so?" Rhys says to her.

"It's not an option," Peter says. "Not until we know what she's done to Sequel."

"Sequel is dead," Nina replies. The skin under her left eye twitches. She grabs at the black hair growing over her ear and twists it between two fingers. Sequel used to twist her hair like that when she lied. Maybe I do it too.

"If Sequel is truly gone, then why should we let you live?" I say.

Nina smiles, drawing it out. I didn't know my face was capable of making a smile that sinister.

"Answer her," Rhys says. "Or I'll come over there and tear your arms off."

"Because," Nina says, standing up slowly. She stretches, arching her back like a cat. "Because if you come at me, I'll have enough time to speak the words."

Sweat breaks out all over my body. Somehow, I know

exactly what words she's talking about. A few simple words took Sequel away and gave us this new girl.

I can't ask her, but Peter can. "What words?"

"The words that will awaken me inside your Miranda too."

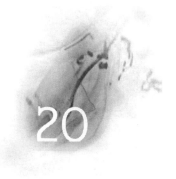

20

"She's *lying*," Rhys says. His hands are fists, white-knuckled. Peter's fingers trail down the inside of my arm until he reaches my hand. He squeezes once. My head swims, mouth bitter with fear. Everything that came before this doesn't compare to the powerlessness I feel now.

All it takes are simple words. She'll speak a code and my consciousness will be shoved aside and North Iteration 9-A will storm in and use my body.

Rhys is about to explode, but Peter remains calm. He steps forward without fear. This is the animal inside him, the one so confident, sometimes I think it can't be real.

"You don't mean that," Peter says softly. "Say them right now. I dare you."

My throat tightens; what is he doing? This is what he was worried about. But then I see—if I change now, they can control the situation, expecting it, but if I don't, then Nina is lying, and we can stop worrying about it.

He's still ten feet from Nina, but she presses her back against the wall. Part of me wants to rush in and snap her neck. Let's see if she can say the words with my hands around her throat.

"Don't come any closer," she spits.

"Say the words," Peter says. "You need all the help you can get."

She shakes her head, glaring daggers. "No. Maybe I have orders to speak them at a particular moment. Now is not that moment."

I want to say she's bluffing, but it could be true. Yet speaking them now would grant her another ally in the room, wouldn't it? I don't know what to believe.

Noah stands against the bars to my left, staring at me. "Why would she say there's a copy of Nina inside you? What am I missing?"

She's lying. Please let me focus.

I feel him leave my mind. When I look to the bars again, he's gone.

Peter is right in front of her now. He reaches out, slowly, and drops a hand on Nina's shoulder, the way one would when conferring with a close friend. "Stay on this side of the cell, for however long we're in here. If you don't, I'll kill you before anyone else can. Do you understand?"

Killing her would be easier, and safer, but that's Peter. He'll give anyone a fair chance.

Nina seems to consider his words. Then she shoves him away with both hands.

Peter's arms windmill, but he regains balance after a few backward steps. Rhys charges forward and Peter shouts, "Wait!"

Rhys freezes, but it's because I dig my fingers into his arm, holding him back with more of my strength than I care to admit. He doesn't try to shake me off.

Peter turns around and walks back to us. "She understands." He puts his hands on our shoulders and turns us around gently, then guides us across the cage.

"We leave her alive?" Rhys says.

We might as well flip a coin. I try to look at it from Sequel's point of view. She didn't ask for this. She's as much a prisoner as we are, maybe more so.

"For now," Peter says. "Until we're sure Sequel can't be recovered. Would you kill us if we were in the same situation?"

Rhys's face falls. It's the wrong question. He *did* kill his team once, long ago. He did it to keep them from being used by the creators, but it was still murder, and we all know it.

He turns away from us, just slightly, eyes on the floor. Probably remembering what he did. It's another reminder he's not one of us, not in the same way. I can't even imagine how to comfort him. *Don't feel bad, Rhys. You had to kill your team!* Yeah, that wouldn't help.

Peter recovers before it's too late. "I'm not talking about what you did, Rhys. You need to know that. You tried your best to save your friends. I'm talking about if there was still a chance to save *us*. Sequel might still be in there."

Rhys's shoulders relax, just slightly. I let out the breath I was holding. For now, we're still a unit.

"Promise me we'll give her a chance," Peter says to both of us. "We owe her that."

Noah's voice returns. "I don't have a say? Kill her. Before she does to you what she did to me."

You don't mean that. But he does. And I want to agree, because maybe I'm a coward and killing her will make me feel safe, rather than giving the girl we brought into our family a chance to return.

"Okay," I say, thankful it isn't my call.

Rhys sighs through his nose. "Right. Okay." He rubs his eyes. "We should rest for whatever comes next."

"I do mean it," Noah says. "Kill her."

"You don't," I say. Aloud.

Peter settles down against the wall. "What?"

I should tell them the truth.

Rhys sits next to him, and they're both watching me just stand here with my hands clasped together.

"Miranda?" Peter says.

I should tell them the truth, but I'm...embarrassed, I think. It sounds too weird.

Over my shoulder, Nina has her eyes mostly closed now, but they open every few seconds.

Noah stands near the bars, grim-faced. "Tell them. And tell them I say hi. But I can't stay here if you guys are going to talk about me. Creeps me out." He sees me hesitate. "Go on."

So I crouch in front of them and put a hand on each of their knees to support myself, then whisper, "When I took Noah's memories, he...came back."

A moment of blank-faced silence passes. Peter's lips part, just slightly.

"He's here," I say.

"What do you mean, *here*?" Peter says.

"I mean, he's alive. In my head. It's him." Just saying it out loud makes me feel insane.

Peter and Rhys share a look.

"Are you kidding?" Rhys says. "Because that's not funny."

"Why would I joke about this?"

"Tell Rhys that I did in fact steal his socks," Noah says.

"Noah stole your socks," I tell Rhys.

Rhys blinks rapidly, like he's just been punched in the nose. Peter closes his eyes. "Can he hear us?"

"Tell Pete I can hear him just fine. I'm out of here." And just like that, his presence evaporates in my head and I'm alone.

Pressure builds behind my eyes, but I'm done crying, even if I just gave Peter more of a reason to distrust me. After all, anytime he speaks to me, Noah could be listening. "He says hi. He just disappeared. He—he comes and goes."

"What does that mean?" Rhys says, too loudly. But Nina doesn't stir.

"It means he's still alive," Peter says, hushed. He almost glares at me now. "I told you not to copy his memories. I told you to let me do it."

"If you had, you'd be in the same position. I can handle this."

I hope I can handle this.

Noah is alive, in a way, and that's the end of it. Rhys squeezes my knee once—the closest he gets to a comforting gesture—and then settles onto his side, using his hands as a pillow. After a moment, Peter pulls me down and rests my head in his lap, automatically taking first watch without discussion. I think I love him because he drops it. He doesn't ask if I'm all right, or if I can handle it. He's just *there*. His fingers stroke my hair and tuck a strand behind my ear. He has me in this position to be close to me. I can feel that. But I wonder if he's thinking what I'm thinking, too. That this is the best position to break my neck if I wake up as someone else.

I dream awful, terrible things.

Then the huge iron door slams open, and I spring upright so fast my feet leave the ground. I come down in a balanced stance with my hands up, but there's no immediate danger. Commander Gane looms outside our cell, still weaponless in his black combat gear, though I guess he doesn't need any. Across the cage, Nina is on her feet.

"The two girls come with me."

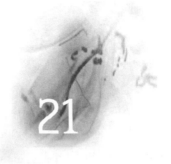

21

The cell door swings open on its own. Nina and I share a look.

Peter and Rhys are wrecked from probably the worst sleep they've ever had, but they're up with me, standing to my left and right.

"I'll be fine," I say, because it's the only thing to say.

"I won't ask again," Gane says. He didn't really ask the first time, but whatever.

Nina walks out of the cage first and turns her head to make sure I won't rush her from behind. I follow her at a safe distance. Safe for her or safe for me, I'm not sure.

"Look sharp," Noah says, suddenly at my elbow. "Nina is going to make a move. I know it."

Are you guessing?

"No, it's like before, when I showed you those images and had no idea where they came from. I can't explain how I know what I know, but I know she's after the Torch, and she can't get it as a prisoner. I'll be around."

He disappears, and I follow Gane into the tunnel, speeding up until I'm shoulder to shoulder with Nina. I want to show her exactly how much I'm not afraid of her, which of course means I am. We're both stiff, less from lack of sleep and more from anxiety. The medieval-style torches flicker and throw our shadows onto the walls.

"Relax, both of you," Gane says without looking back. "I'm not leading you anywhere too sinister." Humor? I can't tell if that's good or bad.

He shows us his back, and I recognize it as a taunt now. It says *Try me.*

Nina does, just like Noah said she would. She lashes out with the same punch I would've done, right on the base of his spine, but she adds her second fist to strike his kidney too, in a double punch. Both blows would send any man to his knees.

They never land. Her knuckles stop a few inches from Gane's back and he makes a clucking sound with his tongue. It's impossible. Her hands just *stopped.*

"I wondered which of you would move against me first."

Nina's hands rise slowly, fingers outstretched and wide, shaking. She's not controlling them, but somehow *he* is.

She stares at them like they're covered in spiders. *"What are you doing?"*

Her left index finger bends backward. I freeze.

"Should I snap it off?" Gane says.

"No! No!" Sweat beads her brow.

Gane gives me a lazy look. "Should I?"

I swallow. Nina looks at me, panic twisting her face. "No," I say.

Her hands tremble as she fights his grip. Her finger is bent past the point of looking natural. Another few degrees and the bone will snap.

"No," I say again, but have no idea why.

Gane releases her, and she clutches both hands to her chest with a moan. He starts away. "Hurry, please."

I follow him, leaving Nina behind. She catches up, and we enter the cavernous main room, the beehive where they pulled me out of the water. The catwalks make it hard to see how many circular levels there are above us. "This is the Verge," Gane says. "It was created to guard against whatever comes through the Black, which is directly under our feet." Automatically I look at the floor. "Anything that comes through is immediately our prisoner."

We stay quiet. Even though I want to ask what exactly could come through the Black.

He leads us to the main pillar in the middle. As we get closer, an elevator door opens at the base of the pillar. Gane steps inside and we follow him, even if entering the cramped space with these two goes against every natural instinct I have. Nina puts her back to the wall, but I face the door and pretend I'm not worried about a thing. Sometimes faking confidence breeds the real thing.

The elevator rises so fast my knees bend and blood rushes out of my head. A few seconds later the doors open and we step into a pyramid-shaped room, the four walls angled to a point high above.

Each wall is glass. I've been in a room like this before, in Mrs. North's memory. The Original Miranda had an office in the shape of a pyramid, with glass walls, but it can't be the same place.

I step into the room.

Each wall is glass, but what I'm seeing through them isn't right.

"This is your first time seeing it," Gane says behind me. I'm vaguely aware of him and Nina stepping around me. The elevator retracts into the floor, giving me a perfect view in all directions.

But I don't understand.

"Are these windows?" They could be video screens. They have to be.

If these are windows, then the Verge is located in the middle of New York City. But the city is not the city I know from my training. We had to memorize the layouts of every major city. The skyline is off—the only thing I recognize is the Empire State Building to the east. The skyscrapers could be a thousand years old, black with age, windowless, crumbling. The sky is dark with a storm. None of the buildings have lights. They are just dark, silent shapes rising up around us, almost invisible in the dim light. To the southwest, I recognize the wedge shape of the Flatiron Building, but it's in the wrong place. It should be to the southeast. This is a joke.

"They're windows," Gane replies.

"No," I reply, because what else can I say? I take a step forward, changing my angle, hoping to see something that will give away the illusion.

Above, the sky is thick with coal-black storm clouds from horizon to horizon. The clouds flash with thick, curling veins of purple lightning.

"A neat trick," I say, almost too quietly for Gane to hear. "Make it go away."

"Would that I could," he says.

Gane walks to a large desk at the north end of the room. He sits down behind it and folds his hands on the smooth wooden surface. There are no chairs for me and Nina. We all flicker purple with the lightning flashes overhead. No thunder comes, and no rain.

"Who are you?" Gane says. He seems to be asking both of us.

Nina speaks first. "It doesn't matter. My offer to remove the eyeless from your world is what matters."

I feel like a poker player without the right cards. I have nothing to offer him, and his face seems to brighten whenever Nina brings up taking the eyeless away.

"You tried to assault me a few minutes ago," he says.

"Can you blame me for attempting to escape?"

Gane ignores her. "And you," he says to me. "Does your sister really know the location of the Torch?"

I glance at Nina, but she's facing forward, staring out at the dead skyscrapers that aren't quite right.

"What is this?" I say.

"Answer me, and then I'll tell you."

It's hard to breathe now.

"Answer me," he says again. "Does she know where the Torch is?"

Maybe the truth will set me free.

"I don't know. And she's not my sister."

Gane frowns. "That's where I'm confused," he says. "It's clear you're not on the same side here."

"We're not," I say. Now he gets it. "Where are we?"

He opens a drawer in his desk and pulls out a crystal carafe filled with a ruby red liquid, wine, most likely. He pours it into a small glass and takes a sip.

"What do you call yourself?" he says to Nina. "Are you a North as well?"

"In a way. My name is Nina."

Not in a good way. Although I guess I don't have any more claim to my name than she does.

"Nina North," he says, tasting the words. "Tell me where you would take these eyeless."

"Through the Black."

I shiver inwardly at the word, but keep myself still. Taking the eyeless anywhere sounds like a bad idea. Killing them is a better one. I see again the images Noah showed me. I see their corpse-pale bodies and the enormous claws they have instead of fingers. I try to recall their faces, but it's too blurry. Letting Nina live was a bad idea. That was our chance to stop this, and we were too weak, all of us. I doubt Gane will give me a second chance to end her.

Gane steeples his fingers. "You said that before. What I want to know is where the Black leads."

"Does it matter?"

Gane nods. "It does to me, yes. The eyeless have ravaged our world. I won't have it done somewhere else just so we can live free of their threat."

"Your world," I say. "This is your world."

He lifts one eyebrow. "Does it look like yours?"

"No. So, *I ask again*, where am I?"

"What's left of my world."

"How did I get here?"

"How can you not know?"

"Because I jumped through a black lake thing and woke up in your cell."

"You came through the Black."

"Which is what, exactly?"

"The boundary between all universes. A buffer, to keep them separate."

I don't say anything.

"Look around you." He takes a sip and gestures with the glass, as if to say, *Go on, take a look. I'll wait.*

I have to believe, because the proof is all around me. This city is as dead and empty as can be.

I can't imagine how it got this way.

He stares at me blankly until I say, "Then where did these eyeless come from? What did they do?"

"They ate," he says, as if that explains it; then to Nina he says, "What guarantee do I have that you won't use the Torch to destroy us completely?"

None, I want to tell him. *Anything that comes out of her mouth is probably a lie. Trust her at your peril.*

Nina raises her hands to the city around us. "What's left to destroy? The eyeless have done a thorough enough job, I think."

"Then why take them?" he says.

Nina has nothing to say.

Gane looks at his desk for several seconds. "I'm going to tell you a story. Will you listen?"

I can't tell who he's talking to, so I just nod, and so does Nina.

"Once there was a park in the city. You can see it just to the north, behind me. Parents took their children there to play. It was full of museums and restaurants, a huge park, right in the middle of everything. They called it, unsurprisingly, Central Park. Until one day in 1973, when a hole opened in the ground and many people fell inside and disappeared. The hole was so black, it was like looking into nothingness. They put tall fences around the hole because they didn't know how to make it go away. Aside from those missing, life went on."

He pauses for another drink. Every hair on my body stands on end.

"When I was a boy, they told me the Black was a gate

to hell. A gate that, if left unguarded, nightmarish creatures would come through. They would beguile and deceive. They would rend the flesh from your bones. Our city was great then, even if the rest of the world was not. We thought New York was invincible. My family came here on a plane from Belize, despite the hole. I remember seeing it through the window as we flew over." He closes his eyes and sighs.

"Then one day things did come through the Black, but they didn't beguile or deceive. They just killed and ate. Creatures with no eyes, mouths filled with needles, claws that could cut a man in two with one swipe. They spread through the city like cancer, cutting people down by the thousands. Thousands became millions. They spread and multiplied. They ate the people of this world and there was no way to stop them. We fought back in a great war that lasted many years. It blackened our land and almost left us extinct. In the end the world was dead and the savaged survivors gathered here. And one day the eyeless just . . . disappeared. They went to the hills, and who knows what they've been doing since. They come to us whenever we have too many children and it seems we might thrive again. They take them and devour them before our eyes. And then they leave us be. Again and again. In the beginning it seemed as if the eyeless moved with one consciousness, controlled by some higher power. Theory turned to fact when the president offered a reward to kill the Torchbearer—a masked woman who was spotted behind the eyeless ranks, holding some kind of staff with the end aflame. The Torch hasn't been spoken of in twenty years, until *you* came through the Black. And now you claim to know where it is."

Commander Gane has tears in his eyes. I know what it's like to remember something you'd rather forget.

"So if you are planning to take them somewhere, I want to know it's not to a world like ours once was. I want to know it's to a hell where the monsters rightfully belong."

22

Gane finishes and sinks into his chair. He pulls out a rag from his vest pouch and mops sweat from his brow.

I stay on my feet, but just barely. The implications . . . it's too much. This was once New York—not mine, but close enough. I try to imagine the monsters spreading and multiplying, eating everything in their path. How do you fight a war against something like that? It's a virus on a global scale.

We've been waiting for these monsters to come and conquer our world. But they've already done it to this world, decades ago. Noah somehow knows what they look like, so they have to be related to the creators. They have to be the monsters Mrs. North was so afraid of.

But the question *why?* remains unanswered. Why destroy this world?

Why destroy ours?

If our world is in the same danger that destroyed Gane's world, then the creators have to be from a different universe entirely. One much more advanced.

Gane folds his rag and takes another drink. "So I ask you for the last time, where do you plan to take the eyeless?"

I speak quickly, before Nina can start. "She's going to use them to conquer our world. She wants to make our world like yours." I know it's true. It all adds up. Nina knew where the entrance to the Black was, and she came here willingly. She wants to control the eyeless, to take them out of *this* world, where their job is clearly finished. It's on to the next world . . . ours.

"She's lying! She's—"

Nina never finishes.

Gane roars and sweeps everything off his desk, bursting upright from his chair. He stretches his hand out to Nina, palm out, fingers spread; Nina chokes as her feet come off the ground. She drifts up . . . then slams hard into the floor. Her head bounces and she writhes on her stomach, moaning.

I don't move.

Because I can't. Gane holds me with his mind the entire time, like a vise. He's crushing my chest, making it hard to breathe. Then he releases me, and my knees wobble and my heart pounds. I start sweating in my burlap bag of an outfit.

Nina climbs to her feet, cautiously, eyes on the floor. A welt on her cheek grows before my eyes, deepening from red to purple.

"Do you want the eyeless gone or not?" Nina says quietly.

"On my terms, yes," Gane says.

The elevator rises out of the floor behind us.

"Miranda North, I will speak with you later," he says, eyes on Nina though he's speaking to me. "You may rejoin the others."

"Don't let her do it—"

"Go!"

I nod and close my mouth. Until I can get Nina alone, I have to trust that Gane is smart enough to see through her deception. If any monster is here to beguile, it's Nina. I wanted to give Sequel that chance to return, but there's too much at stake now. Too much...

"Go, now," he says, quieter.

I nearly say thank you but realize how pathetic that would be. The fact that I'm about to return to Peter and Rhys is almost enough to make me smile. The only reason I *wouldn't* want to leave is so Nina can't try to manipulate Gane. Who knows what she'll say or do when I'm gone?

In the next second, Noah is standing in front of me, and I

almost yelp. "You can't let her stay with Gane," he says, panicked. "You can't."

Why not?

"Because she's going to trick him. He's underestimating her. Listen, I know things about Nina I shouldn't know. Someone put this information in my head. I think—"

Gane is staring me down. "Leave under your own power, Miranda."

There's nothing I can do.

Noah sighs. "I know."

I turn around and see that the two in red have returned to escort me. The man and girl with their outlaw masks. They're stoic as before, hands clasped behind them, eyes forward but not looking at anything in particular, especially not me.

I step into the elevator and turn around, ready to rejoin Peter and Rhys. Nina and Gane watch as the doors begin to close.

In the last moment, right before the doors shut, Nina turns her head and smiles at me.

Being alone with Gane is exactly what she wants.

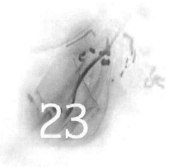

23

We ride down as fast as we ascended. My stomach flutters and my feet go light. I feel their eyes on my back, but refuse to give them the satisfaction of turning around.

I break the silence as we step onto the main floor. "Hey, could you guys fill in the part between my coming through the Black and waking up in that cell with different clothes on?"

I hear the girl's steps falter, then resume.

The man says, "You came through unconscious, which happens for everyone the first time they go through. Your armor was removed for obvious reasons."

His voice sounds familiar, in a way.

It takes everything not to turn around and rip his mask off. We enter the tunnel lined with torches, and their footsteps become crisp. They stay a few paces back, which I'm grateful for.

"Who removed it?" I say.

"I did," the girl says.

"Everyone gets knocked out the first time, huh?"

"Yes," the girl says. I'm surprised they're talking to me at all.

"Who were the other interlopers? The ones who came before us?"

"I was one once," the man says, which makes me stop, but his gentle hand on my back pushes me forward, and my spirits rise with a shred of hope. More from the way he guided me than his words. I wait, not sure what it means.

We pass through the iron door into the jail. Peter and Rhys jump up from where they were resting against the wall.

"What happened?" Peter says, coming to the bars.

But it's the man behind me who answers. "Quiet, all of you." His tone has changed. He's not telling us to shut up because we're prisoners; he's doing it because he doesn't want anyone to hear. My heart thrums. *Please don't let it be a trick.*

Rhys's mouth drops open and his eyes narrow. Behind me, the iron door shuts softly but doesn't lock.

"Take off the mask," Rhys says.

"I said *quiet*," the man in red growls.

The cell door swings open, whether automatically or under the man's power, I don't know. And I don't care.

"Step out," the man says.

The girl hovers by the door, shifting from foot to foot. They're as tense as I am. Which is the only reason I don't think they're acting under Commander Gane's orders.

"Is this a trick?" Rhys says.

If it is, it doesn't make sense. Gane has the power to move us however he wants to. He doesn't need to trick us.

"Boy, I don't have the time or the patience. Follow me, or rot here. Assuming Gane doesn't dismantle you first to see what makes an interloper tick."

Peter and Rhys share a look, then step out of the cage. The two in red whirl around and open the door again. They move fast and so do we. My heart pounds, but not from fear. Even with the horrors that lie outside this building, we have a chance if we're together.

"What about our armor?" Rhys says.

"It's taken care of," the girl says over her shoulder. Up close, her eyes are the color of honey.

"We need something hidden within the suits," Peter adds.

"Taken care of," the man says. It's enough for us to follow him—not like we have an abundance of options.

We exit the tunnel onto the main floor of the beehive, then

start along the perimeter wall, following the circumference of the floor counterclockwise.

Suddenly, Noah is walking beside me. "You sure this is a good idea?" He cranes his head down to peer into my face, but I refuse to look at him.

Nope. But it's the only option I see at the moment.

"Because right now we know where Nina is. If we leave, we might not find her again until it's too late."

If we stay, it's as prisoners.

"Listen, I think I know who Nina really is."

Who?

"You know the Miranda you saw in Mrs. North's memories? The one we think is the Original you?"

Yes. How could I forget? It was the first time we realized that our creators seem to have creators of their own.

"Yeah, I think Nina is her *daughter*. A clone the director raised as her own child."

The director?

I almost stop to look at him, but we're moving too fast.

"Almost there," the man says from the front. We're approaching the next tunnel cut into the wall.

That's when the elevator door in the pillar opens and Commander Gane steps out, Nina at his side.

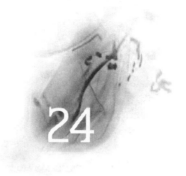

24

"Where are you taking them?" Gane calls from the pillar. No alarm in his voice, not yet. With each passing second, I expect to feel his mind grab my body, to hold me in place.

"Don't stop," the girl hisses at us.

The man breaks off from our group and faces Gane. "Commander, the scientists wish to study the interlopers in their laboratory."

Footsteps clack on the stone floor—Gane walking toward us, fast. "No, no no no. No one moves them without my permission. Take them back."

By now we're halfway into the tunnel.

"Stop!" he yells. I feel the first brush of his mind against my skin. It evaporates the second I'm out of his sight.

"Run!" the girl says, sprinting ahead. "The horses know the way!"

Horses?

I don't have time to think about it. Peter and Rhys fly past me, and I coax a little more strength from my limbs until I'm running just as fast. Faster, even. A hiss carries down the tunnel from behind, and I recognize the sound—smoke grenade. Over my shoulder, a wall of gray smoke billows after us. The man in red bursts through it, arms pumping.

"Gane's blinded!" he shouts. "Keep moving."

He doesn't have to tell us twice. The tunnel slopes down, around a corner, then up again to the exit. I'm almost giddy with the freedom of open sky above me, even though it's not my sky. I catch the landscape in a glance—ancient rotting skyscrapers, the towering sharp beehive of the Verge surrounded by a moat of black water. The tunnel traveled under the moat and let us out at the water's edge.

Like the girl said, five horses wait just ahead in the street, next to the burned-out hulk of what was once a taxi. They stamp their feet and churn up dust with their hooves. The man types a code into the keypad outside the tunnel's opening and a portcullis slams down.

"What is this?" Rhys says, head craned back at the ruin around us. *"What—?"*

"Shut up. He can still grab us," the man says, breathless. "Take a horse."

Four of the horses are all black. The last one is gray, but only because of the dust and grit matted in her coat. Patches of her shine through brilliant white. None of them have saddles.

Peter and Rhys are slow to move toward the horses, obviously stunned by their surroundings.

"Now!" the man roars.

The gray one turns her eye to me, as much of an invitation as I'll get. I grab a hank of her mane and swing my leg up and over.

Smoke pours through the bars in the portcullis. I hear Gane coughing in the cloud, much too close.

"Dammit, boy!" The man circles his black horse past Rhys, who refuses to climb on. Not the best time for his trust issues to surface. Peter and his horse are already twenty yards down the street, the Empire State Building towering behind him. He stops and swings the horse around, mouth falling open. I follow his gaze—

The last free horse whinnies as its hooves come off the ground. It hovers under Gane's power, legs thrashing at the air. My gray steps sideways, nimble as a dancer, as the black throws its head around, wide-eyed, lips pulling back from its teeth as Commander Gane lifts it higher. I grab the gray's mane with both hands as she shifts under me. She rears, kicking with her front legs, and comes down, but she doesn't leave the other horses behind, even with my frantic heels digging into her side.

"Go girl!" I plead.

Gane is at the bars, choking on the smoke cloud, hand stretched through with fingers spread wide. He snaps his wrist like he's tossing a chip into his mouth, and the horse arcs up and over the mouth of the tunnel like a tossed football. I watch, frozen, as it plunges into the black moat.

Rhys decides it's time to go right about then.

"Ride!" the man shouts. The girl in red blows past me, and Peter's black horse kicks up a plume of dust as he keeps the lead. Rhys scrambles onto the back of the man's horse, and together we pound the dirt, side by side. My horse moves under me like liquid, carrying me away from Gane and the Verge. I feel Gane's mind crawl over my skin, tugging at my rags and limbs. I begin to rise off the gray, but clamp my feet down at the last second. She seems to run faster as I settle onto her back again.

And then we're out of range, with a cloud of dust two stories high rising between the buildings, eclipsing the Verge.

Gane's scream of frustration echoes off the steel and glass, disturbing crows roosting in the broken windows. They take flight, crisscrossing over us, cawing. And I'm laughing, not because I'm happy, but because I'm out in the open, free. Wind tears at my hair and makes my eyes water. Eventually the man, with Rhys holding on behind him, takes the lead, and we follow him as he winds through the dusty paths between buildings. I'm grateful for the action, as it gives me a break from thinking, from trying to understand how this place is possible.

I see the remains of the city as we pass. An orange-brown lump of metal that used to be a car here. Broken, pebbled pieces of blacktop there. Wide gray streaks of dust border some of the buildings, the powdered remains of sidewalks. We pass the north side of the Empire State Building; fires burn within, dark shapes crouched around them. A twisted, half rusted sign on the ground says 5 AV.

People huddle in the doorways of buildings, watching as we pound past. I'm not laughing anymore. I look at a world near death and realize this could happen to us. Nina wants to take the eyeless through the Black, and as far as I know, the Black leads to our world.

It makes me want to go back for her, but I don't. We're not ready. The two in red broke us out for a reason, and I assume they're willing to help.

More people come out of their dwellings to watch.

A cry rises up, carried ahead of us. "Red riders! Red riders!"

"Don't stop!" the man shouts next to me. "Just don't stop!" We're at full gallop, a storm of hooves louder than thunder, drowning out the thump of blood in my veins. I feel my gray breathing beneath me, the muscles in her back flexing each time her legs come off the ground.

"Keep going!" the man shouts.

As the arrows begin to fall.

They come from above. Ragged men lean out from the broken windows on the second and third and fourth floors of the buildings. The cry in the street is no longer *"Red riders!"* but *"Meat!"* and the arrows zip down from the left and right, cracking into the hard-packed dirt or ricocheting off chunks of blacktop. One grazes my horse's shoulder and she jumps, almost throwing me off her back. I grasp her mane tighter, squeezing with my legs, hunching, trying to make myself two dimensions.

Another comes right at my face. No thought—I lean, and it passes through my hair, severing a lock. I feel the strands flutter down my back, then catch in the wind. My stomach clenches long after the arrow is gone, things moving too fast for me to process.

The girl in red has one in her thigh, but by the way she rides you wouldn't know it. The red fabric of her pants is darker around the wound, and the stain is growing. I close my eyes, waiting for one to pierce my neck, wishing I had my armor. Then I open them, because wishing isn't going to get us through this.

The men are terrible shots, but numerous. The arrows continue to whistle down, buried shafts snapping under hooves.

I see an archer aim for Peter from the second floor on the left. His neck is wrapped in a filthy towel, thin arms straining against the bow. He tracks Peter as we approach his building.

"Peter, watch out!" My voice is drowned in the roar of hooves.

The archer fires. The arrow flies down, wobbling, and sinks into the chest of Peter's horse.

25

I open my mouth to scream but no sound comes out. The horse collapses, head slamming the ground, legs tangled under it, skidding, churning up dirt. Peter skids with it and then tumbles.

Two more arrows stab into the dirt near his head. Somehow he turns his second tumble into a controlled forward roll. He pops to his feet and reaches up. And I'm there, leaning down off my horse at near full gallop, all my focus on his outstretched fingers, knowing I won't get a second chance at this. Our hands collide with our forearms, and his weight almost pulls me off, but I bite down with my legs and swing him up, screaming against the pain in my shoulder.

The arrows are out of range finally. Peter's chest heaves

against my back as he takes deep gulps of air. I hear Rhys laughing from ahead. My shoulder is on fire, but intact.

"I owe you one," Peter says in my ear.

I twist around to look at him, checking for arrows he might not be feeling yet. His eyes blaze with adrenaline.

"That's two you owe me," I say, and he laughs.

We ride on, deeper into the city. We pass wild dogs with stark rib cages. More cars are skewed in the road. The tires rotted away long ago. The horses stay clustered, breaking apart only to get around an obstacle. As the adrenaline fades, more of what I'm seeing makes its way to my brain. So many things made by man, long forgotten and abandoned. People walked these sidewalks, ate in these restaurants. Cabs once packed the desolate roads. And behind everything is a possible future for my world. If we don't stop Nina, this will be our future. A world of forgotten things.

Our pace slows after ten minutes of hard riding. We turned south a while back, and the buildings became slightly shorter, but just as dense. Every few blocks the angle is right, and I can see Gane's version of downtown in the very far distance. I can't tell what's different.

The girl's leg is soaked now, but the bleeding seems to have stopped. The stain doesn't go past her knee. Dust sticks to the wet part of her pants.

The street opens up into what was once a park. Some of the trees still stand, and one of them even looks alive. The rest sag, leafless, anchored in baked dirt. We ride the perimeter, staying clear of a hollow bus. Two buzzards perch at the front of the metal hulk, watching us.

"This is what you would know as Union Square," the man in red says. "Here it was named Rowland Circle." He takes the lead, guiding his horse into an enormous parking garage that has fared better than the buildings around it. We follow him inside and begin the descent, curling around pillars, heading deeper underground. The cars here are better preserved, but just barely. None of them have tires or windows. Every few feet, the man stops and holds a small remote in the air. The remote beeps, and we move on.

I count three levels down until the sounds from above are muffled and all I hear are the too-loud claps of our horses' hooves on concrete. The bottom level is an apartment. Two cots are tucked in the far left corner, alongside a huge metal desk, cabinets, and a workbench. Various mismatched lamps hang from the supports in the ceiling, strung together with wire. Hay covers the ground right next to us, with a trough for water. In the middle of everything is a fire pit dug into the concrete.

I see it all, but I don't understand. I already knew the two in red aren't who they appear to be, but why bring us here?

Part of me stays alert, but I release my doubt for a moment and focus instead on the warmth of Peter against my back.

"If you decide to leave, please let me know in advance so I can deactivate the security." The man slips from his horse. He hasn't yet removed his mask. He crosses to the girl and studies the arrow in her leg. "Ah, we should've stopped."

"Too close to the Verge," she replies, wincing as his fingers barely touch the arrow shaft.

"You said you had our armor," Rhys says, now alone on the horse he had shared. He does something with his feet and the horse takes a few steps back. "And I hope you have answers."

The mention of our armor and the memory of what they contain is like a soft punch to the stomach. We have to be cutting it close on our memory shots.

Peter swings his leg off our horse and stands between me and Rhys.

"I said it was taken care of," the man says. "Patience."

Peter takes a step forward before Rhys's mouth can get us into more trouble. "With respect, we don't have any patience left. We're running out of time. If we don't get to our armor, we're going to lose our memories. Do you understand?"

The man sighs and looks up at the girl, who I can see clearly now that we've stopped moving. She's pulled the mask down around her throat. Her dark skin is flawless, which surprises me considering the world she lives in. Her face is thin and almost undernourished, and she doesn't fill out her combat uniform. None of this keeps her from being beautiful. It's stupid, but I immediately look at Peter to see if he's studying her the way I am.

"Sophia, can you handle your wound?" the man says.

She nods curtly. The man helps her off the horse, then watches her limp toward the open cabinets at the other end of the apartment. "You all right?" he calls after her. She just waves a hand behind her, keeps limping.

The man turns to us and pulls down his mask.

My mouth falls open.

He's blond like Rhys, hair growing to the base of his neck, but I already knew that. His blond beard is short but thick. His irises are red, something I didn't notice before. His face is what Rhys's will look like many years from now.

Rhys makes a sound I've never heard him make before. A soft exhale of surprise.

The man smiles up at Rhys, and his lined eyes twinkle with tears.

"Hello, son," he says.

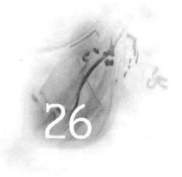

26

Rhys can't speak.

None of us can. No one says a word for what feels like a minute. Rhys's eyes are shiny. He never talked about his "father." Rhys was part of the first Alpha team, the one a year ahead of ours. The creators raised and trained Rhys's team themselves, as their children. Then one day Rhys's father just disappeared. Rhys assumed his father had been killed. Instead he ended up here, working in the Verge. . . .

"Where are we?" I say. Not that it isn't crazy to see this guy in the flesh now, but we have bigger problems. And I'm guessing he has answers.

Rhys Noble—I remember Rhys telling me his father's name—takes a long breath. "The short answer is another universe. One of many."

If someone tells you you're in another universe, it's hard to go, *Oh, makes sense now.* But instead of disbelief, I feel nothing. Another universe. Okay.

"My name is Rhys. You can call me Noble, to avoid confusion. As in my last name, not because I possess outstanding qualities." He leads Sophia's horse to the trough. I dismount, and my horse follows automatically. "The girl is Sophia," he says. "She's of this world." Noble waits until Rhys robotically dismounts, then leads the last horse to the trough. "But let's take care of your immediate situation."

We follow Noble to one of the cabinets, where he pulls out our suits. The scaled black material is folded neatly. He hands one to each of us and says, "Leave your reserve shots in your suits, please. I have more. In the pouches you'll find the tracking devices you had in your suits."

On the workbench is a glass case full of syringes. Each one is filled with the lemonade-colored liquid I'm so familiar with. Noble lifts the lid.

Our memory shots, but not the ones we brought with us.

"Why do you . . . ?" Rhys says, but he's still stunned. His face is slack and emotionless.

"When I saw who came through the Black, I made a batch," Noble says, opening the case and pulling out three syringes.

Behind Noble, Sophia eases the arrow out of her thigh. She bites her lip and looks at the ceiling. The bloodstain on her pants spreads past her knee.

"Where is Noah?" Noble asks me.

Suddenly he's there at my side, in his armor. He needs to stop popping up like this; I can't take it.

No one speaks.

"That's too bad," Noble says. "I'm sorry. I'd given him something to help your team."

"What did you give him?" I ask, as Noah says, "What did he give me?"

Noble picks up a rag off the bench and wipes his hands. "Six months ago I went into your world. I came across Noah in the woods outside Tycast's base, and I incapacitated him. Then I implanted in him a directive to stop Nina if she ever showed up, accompanied by information and history that would help him—and all of you—to complete that task. I knew it was only a matter of time."

Noah shakes his head. "I can't remember. Tell him I said hi, and that he's a dick because he didn't have to knock me out."

"Noah says hi," I say. "I downloaded his memories and now his consciousness is in my head. So."

Noble actually gasps. "That's extraordinary." He sees my face. "I'm sorry, I shouldn't have said that. But the implications...I had posited that two minds could share the same brain, but...Does he remember any of the information I gave him?"

"Bits and pieces," I say. "He showed me what the Torch looks like."

"Noble," Peter says impatiently. "Let's get to it. What are we?"

"I'm afraid we're all the same thing," Noble says. "Clones."

"Explain," Peter says.

"I'll be fifty years old in the spring," Noble says. "Yet the person I was cloned from looks no older than eighteen—like you, Rhys—and has lived for close to a thousand years. All of you have an Original too. The five of them make up the ruling body of the most powerful universe in the Black, called True Earth." He looks at each of us and seems to be satisfied we're getting it. His words are like bombs going off in my head.

"I was sent to your world decades ago, as a boy, with my team, to age, to learn the ways of your specific society, and to raise a group of soldiers—that's you—who would become a new generation of peacekeepers in the world. Only that was a lie told to us by *our* creators. Instead of peace, there would be war. The teams we raised would lead the vanguard of an army when it came time to purge your world. How's that?"

We were going to be the tip of the spear.

"Huh," Rhys says.

Noble says, "Priority. Take your shots."

We take them. The familiar sting in my arm is welcome. Noble studies us. It's not a smart thing, taking drugs from a stranger, but there isn't much choice.

"So what is the Black?" Rhys says.

Noble smiles, and it's easy to see the scientist in him. "Think of the Black like a honeycomb, each universe cradled in a cell. It works as a lubricant, like how oil keeps two pieces of metal from grinding together."

That should rock me, but after everything I just try to absorb it. It's hard, because I'm stuck on this one idea. I'm thinking that if this is all there is, this endless journey of fighting and insane revelations, I'm in trouble. If the rest of my life is going to be devoted to fighting, I'm not sure I want that. No matter what I was made for.

"Let them dress, Noble," Sophia says. She takes her vest off, then eases her pants down over her wound. She's wearing two wide strips of cloth to cover herself. Her muscles are hard and lean, like an animal pared down to the essentials. I watch the way she moves to see if she's dangerous, if she could take us. Rhys watches for another reason.

"Of course," Noble says. "I'm sure you'll feel better in your armor."

"Sure," Rhys says absently.

I walk up to the next level of the parking garage and take off my rags and toss them against the wall. Then I step into my armor, and I feel safe again, even if I'm not.

On the way back I see Peter and Rhys changing. Rhys still looks dazed and doesn't notice me, but Peter does as he pulls his armor over his hips. He doesn't slide his arms through his sleeves right away. He smiles at me, as warm as can be under the circumstances. My cheeks grow hot and so does my stomach, and it's so good to feel something besides terror and anguish. I reach out and trail my fingers over his bare back. His skin is blazing, almost feverish. Then the moment is gone and I remember where we are.

When we get back to the living area, Noble is rummaging through a cabinet. Sophia has finished stitching the wound in her leg. She bends the limb back and forth, making sure the stitches won't tear. Rhys watches her until she looks up and furrows her brow. Noah stands in front of Rhys, waving a hand in front of his face.

Noble stands up holding a memory band. "I thought it might be better to show you how I got here. And what we're up against."

No one speaks.

"Who wants to go first?" he says.

"Me," I say. I'm sick of waiting for the truth.

I lie down on the nearest cot, and Noble slides the band over my head.

It doesn't even hurt this time.

27

I open my eyes and find they belong to Rhys Noble, but something is different. There's no emotion. I am not partially becoming the person, like I did with Mrs. North and Rhys and Noah. It's like Noble removed his private thoughts and only the visuals remain.

Noble sits at a desk inside an office. Through his eyes I see him scrawling something on a notepad. Some kind of formula. The door opens, but he keeps scratching out numbers and letters.

"Thank you for knocking," he says.

He finishes writing, then looks up. And freezes. A woman stands in front of his desk, wearing a dark hooded vest and a mask over her nose and mouth. Her face is in deep shadow.

"Can I help you?" he says.

"Rhys Noble, you are a man of reason and logic. I am short on time. Do not speak until I am done. Do you understand me?"

"Yes," Noble says.

"There was another world like this," she begins. "They had people and cars and a blue sky and vast oceans."

Noble sits in utter silence, listening to the intruder as she tells him about a world, Gane's world, that was a little more advanced than ours. They were on the moon in 1941, Mars in 1949. The world grew, and soon the people were living too long. Then they were living indefinitely, and the planet's population began to grow impossibly fast. Scientists were dangerously close to discovering the Black . . . and the means to travel through it. Wars I've never heard of broke out—the Indian War, and the War at Home, which turned into the American War. It ravaged the lands and made clean water scarce.

One day a hole opened in Central Park. It was 1973.

At this point I remember something Mrs. North said to me, just seconds before I escaped her.

"There is no escaping True Earth," she told me.

True Earth had decided that Gane's world had grown too

big, too powerful, too corrupt, too advanced. They were considered a threat. Aggressive worlds with means to travel through the Black would not be tolerated. The people still fought in wars over menial things like land or religion—something True Earth had done away with centuries ago. So True Earth sent the eyeless through and pared the world down to the basics again. The plan was to remove the humans in such a way that left the world unharmed. After all, what was the point of conquering a world if you left it in ruins? Except the humans fought back with weapons that blackened the sky and scorched the land. Then they died, and the eyeless went to the hills until they were needed for the next world.

The woman goes out of focus slightly, and I realize Noble is tearing up. "Bullshit. We're here to bring peace to this world. These kids are going to *end war*."

"They're going to *make war*," the woman says. "True Earth sent you here almost forty years ago to start the process that will cleanse your world. You grew up here to learn its intricacies. Your Roses grew up here for the same reason."

"I don't believe you. Who are you?"

She ignores him. "It's a new tactic, Noble, that's all. We lost the last world to war. This one will be ripe for resettlement. The Roses will herd the population with fear, then the eyeless will kill them efficiently. No war, just slaughter. Like herding sheep for wolves. And once the psychic energy fades, only a pristine, human-free world will remain. Most importantly, the world will no longer be a threat to True Earth."

"Why are they doing this?" Noble says. He believes her now. I can hear the resignation in his voice.

"To make sure they are the only world worth anything. That no one will ever challenge them for space or resources. To make sure no world surpasses them or threatens their control, for they believe no world is better suited to lead or police. The world with the blackened sky I spoke of was not the first to die, and it won't be the last. Like the last world, your people are seen as corrupt, fighting over natural resources and religion. But even if none of that were true, your society is advancing at a rate that will soon make the discovery of the Black possible, which they fear because you'll be able to reach out and touch them."

She takes a step forward.

"I am here because your world is next, Rhys Noble. I am one of the ruling five of True Earth."

"Then why are you telling me this? Who are you? You're not Miranda. . . . You're . . ."

She holds her hands out, palms up. A welcoming gesture. "You know my name."

Noble shakes his head. "Take off the mask."

The woman sighs and pulls down her hood, revealing a cascade of black hair. Then she tugs the mask down around her neck. She's not a woman at all, but a girl of about seventeen. "Do you know me now?"

"Yes. Hello, Olivia." Noble's tone changes, as if he's suddenly realized he's talking to royalty.

It's like seeing a ghost in the flesh. I can't help but relive the moment my Olive caught a bullet in the crown of Key Tower. She was dead before any of us knew what happened. She deserved more.

"I helped put you into this world, Noble. But now I want to help you save it. I'm gathering people to fight back. Do you know the role the Original Miranda has in my world?"

"She's the director of True Earth. I've never met her. I've never met any of you. We were just *put* here, with a mission you're now telling me is false."

"The director already has an agent among you," Olivia says. "One who knows the truth. Who do you trust the least?"

"Miranda," he says without hesitation. "Mrs. North, the kids call her." He rubs at his temples and takes a deep breath. "I haven't trusted her since we were kids."

"Then your instincts are correct. The director only trusts her own clones. Not even me, and I'm nearly her equal."

"My colleagues," Noble says. "Do they know the truth?"

"I can't be sure who is and who isn't aware of your true purpose."

"And my Original? The Rhys I come from?"

"He is like the others. I am the only one fighting back, in secret."

Olivia lifts her hood and settles it on her head. She pulls a black, bulky glove from her pocket and wiggles her left hand into it. Then she kneels and points her finger near the floor, like she's pressing an invisible button six inches off the ground. The glove gives off a metallic, high-pitched whine. Rising, she draws a fast circle in the air, kneeling again to complete the shape. A black hole snaps into existence, with no sound, inside the border of the circle she drew. Staring into it gives me vertigo. It is utter emptiness and infinity at the same time. It is the Black.

"Come with me," she says.

The Black hovers for several moments before Noble moves. It doesn't vibrate or shimmer; it just waits for them, a patient mouth that feels older than time itself.

Finally Noble rises and crosses the room. Olive takes his hand, and together they step through.

The next second, Noble is standing on the sidewalk in a city I now recognize. I see the blackened sky, the ruined streets. This is Gane's New York.

Noble swears softly. "What is this?"

"The future of your world, if you do nothing."

"Why me?" Noble says.

In the middle of an intersection up ahead, I see two human-shaped things hunched over something in the road. A dead deer, it looks like. Their skin is milk-white.

The two creatures notice Noble and Olivia. They go perfectly still.

"Why me?" Noble says again. "Jesus, what are those things?"

"Why you? Because of all the Originals, Rhys gives Miranda the most trouble. He's the most combative and the least likely to agree with her. I wondered if I might find that in you. It wasn't until I got to your office that I was sure you were uncorrupted."

"What do I do?" he says quickly. He looks at the Black behind him, as if checking to make sure it's still ready for him to leap through. The portal waits patiently.

The two creatures are now coming closer.

"You can't kill your colleague Miranda. She's too well protected for that, as her Original's chosen. And it won't stop what's coming. One day the director will send Nina, the clone she raised as her daughter, to gather the eyeless and join your teams. Then the end will begin."

The eyeless are coming closer now; at first I didn't know it was them, but now I can see their faces.

"Will you join the rebellion?" she asks.

"Yes," Noble says.

28

The memory ends, and I'm back in Noble and Sophia's apartment. It feels like passing from one nightmare into another.

"What did you see?" Peter asks me, but Noble just hands the memory band to him. Once Peter is finished, his blue eyes will be gone forever. But Peter just lies down and slides the band over his head.

"We'll have to get you some contacts, for at home," Rhys says. "You're part of the vampire club now." He's feeding one of the horses some hay.

"I have to see this," is all Peter says. He inhales softly as the machine turns on.

I turn to Noble. "How did you end up working for Gane?"

"Simple," he says. "Olivia got me a place in the Red Guard, which is the police unit that still functions in this world. It's the only place where I can monitor the Black closely. And the last place True Earth would look for me."

He's about to say more when Sophia walks up to us. "Come with me, Miranda," she says. "I need to retrieve something before dusk."

I'm on the gray-white horse, whose name is Axela, walking down a narrow and dusty side street. Sophia walks next to me on her black one, Mockbee. She's swapped her stained and bloodied gear for a new set in the same dusky red. She has a bow across her lap, an arrow already nocked.

What I saw in Noble's memory slowly settles into something I can accept. It's too weird to be anything but true. Out of all the craziness, I'm fixated on how long the Originals have been around. My clone source has been alive since the Dark Ages.

Our enemy has *lifetimes* of experience. How can we compete?

Sophia kicks her horse into a canter. "C'mon," she calls back. "Night falls soon and we don't want to be out then."

No, I imagine we don't.

I catch up to her; the speed increase reminds me of the bruises on my legs and arms and torso—my whole body, really.

Wearing my armor helps a little. "How did you and Noble meet?"

She doesn't say anything for an entire block.

"He found me a few years ago. I wandered down the wrong alley near the market, and three men grabbed me and pulled me into a building." She slows to a trot. "I . . . They tore my clothes off." She clenches her jaw. A moment passes where she seems to harden herself against the memory. "I screamed and kicked and one of them pulled a knife and held it against my eye."

I feel my pulse in the scar on my cheek.

"The leader had his pants down when Noble appeared." Her voice changes to reverence. "He was like a ghost. He moved so fast, he smashed their heads in with a rock before they really knew what was happening. Then he gave me a red robe to cover myself, this ceremonial robe of the Red Guard. And he gave me something to eat." She rubs at her eye. "He sponsored me into the Red Guard program."

We trot for another block.

"Sorry it's not a happy story," she says, but with defiance.

"It has a happy ending," I say.

Soon I hear sounds up ahead. Market sounds.

"Stay close to me and don't make eye contact," Sophia says. "Act like they're beneath you."

We turn the corner and enter what must be the market. It's nearly deserted, just rows of empty stalls in a huge square lot. The perimeter appears to be fenced in at first, but then I see it's just the jagged first floor of a decapitated building. The market is in the footprint of a long-gone skyscraper. About one in every five stalls is occupied, but the people are packing up.

In the distance, a bell rings softly.

"Thirty minutes of light left," she says. "We're okay." That doesn't stop the chill from running back and forth across my shoulders.

The man comes out of the alley to our right. At first I think it's an eyeless because of the hunched posture, but then I see the dark pits of his eyes and the crude blade in his fist. He does his best impression of a run at Sophia's flank, but he's slower than me on a bad day. I tuck my legs under me, stand up on Axela, then leap off, swinging my legs forward in midair. I land with both feet on his chest and take him to the ground. His ribs crack and his mouth opens, sucking at air.

"Leave him," Sophia says over her shoulder.

"I just saved your life," I say, feeling more than a little underappreciated.

"For which I am eternally grateful, but we haven't much time."

The man groans and writhes on the ground. I kick his

blade to the gutter and hop back on my horse. Sophia is already twenty feet ahead, and I don't want to be left behind in this awful place.

Sophia snatches up an apple as she passes a fruit stall. The apple is brownish, and the frail woman behind the stall doesn't say a word. In the same motion, Sophia tosses it down the row to a little girl with matted hair and a dirty face. The girl looks around to make sure no one saw her catch it, then she takes off in the opposite direction.

"Come on," Sophia says when she sees I've lagged behind.

I give Axela a nudge with my heels, and we move to another stall still open for business. A beefy man stands behind it, wearing loose threadbare shirt and pants. His bloodshot eyes flit between Sophia and me.

"Need the batteries today," she says, straight to the point. Even though she hasn't exactly been nice to me, I think I like this girl.

"I tell him it will take a few weeks," the man says with a Russian accent.

"Nonsense," Sophia says, circling Mockbee around his stall. "We've *given* you weeks. Now fulfill your word."

The man smiles, showing brown teeth. "I joke. You have the coin?"

Sophia pulls a small sack off her belt and tosses it to the man. He catches it and tests the weight in his palm. Then he picks up a bag from behind his stall and whips it at her. It's heavy and almost knocks her off her horse.

She slings it over her shoulder. "You're lucky I'm in a hurry."

The man raises a hand wrapped in yellowed bandages. "Okay! Thank you too! Send my regards to the Red Guard, yes?"

Sophia glares at him, then turns Mockbee around and trots away. I follow.

"What are the batteries for?" I say, once we've left the market and are back on the empty roads. The sky is darker now, and the shadows all blend.

"The thing that'll give us a fighting chance."

We're a mile from home when full dark falls. The streets are so black, I can't tell where concrete ends and sky begins. Every few seconds the sky flashes violet and I catch a glimpse of where we are. I see a snapshot of Sophia looking back at me, face drawn tight.

"Ride hard. The horses know the way." And she's off, the next flash showing her horse in full gallop.

"C'mon," I whisper, digging in my heels. Axela responds, and I chase after Sophia.

Over the pound of hooves and my heart, I hear things moan in the buildings we pass. I hear bones breaking, like limbs snapping off a tree. The moans turn to screams, and

I see shapes in the windows and doors and hear sounds like nails on a chalkboard.

"Are you thinking about me?" Noah says in my head.

His sudden voice is a comfort, not a scare this time. I can pretend I'm not alone. Sophia pulls farther ahead. In the next flash I see something in the road between us. . . .

A little boy on his hands and knees.

But it's not a little boy. Where his eyes should be are just smooth planes of flesh. No nose, either, just twin openings above a tiny rosebud mouth. It freezes my blood, and I *feel* Noah's horror flood through me.

"Oh my God . . ." he says.

The eyeless is in full gallop after Sophia's horse. It scrambles over garbage heaps and around collapsed sections of the road.

It gains on her, and I scream "Sophia!" so loud my throat burns.

She swivels on Mockbee and pulls out a slingshot. Metal flashes in the next lightning strike. The eyeless trips and rolls in the dirt; my horse runs directly over it, crushing it under hooves, cutting off its screams.

"Take a left!" Sophia yells back.

I look behind me as lightning flashes again.

Three more eyeless gallop after me. I grip the reins until

194

the leather creaks. Axela leans left into the parking garage entrance and we pound inside. Something buzzes behind me; a red grid of lasers is now in place over the opening. The eyeless run past it, which makes me wonder if they're moving toward another entrance.

"Okay, nice," Noah says. "A laser door. I like laser doors."

Me too.

"Hey," he says. "If you get some privacy later, we need to talk." I feel him recede.

Sophia breathes heavily beside me. "The eyeless know they can't get in, so they give up."

A wave of nausea hits me. "What are they doing in the city?" I say.

Sophia walks her horse down the ramp, and mine follows. "Some of them stay in the city to feed at night. It's the best time for them, since they can see in the dark and we can't."

"How can they see at all?"

"They're psychics. They see everything with their minds. It's literally impossible to hide from them. Once they enter a room, they know where everything is instantly."

Making them the perfect hunter-killers. A chill runs up and down my spine.

"Then where did they come from?" I say.

She doesn't bother to look back. "You with the questions. I

don't know where they came from. Probably from True Earth. They're all the same, all of them. We've caught and killed them, and genetically they're all identical."

"How is that possible?" I say, and then the answer comes to me.

The eyeless are clones.

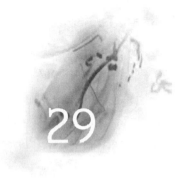

29

A fire burns low in a crater busted out of the concrete, right in the middle of the apartment. A vertical aluminum pipe routs the smoke out of the garage. Sophia hands me a stick with some kind of sizzling meat on it, dripping with juice. I don't ask what it is, just tear a chunk off with my teeth and chew. It tastes so good my knees weaken.

Peter is conferring with Noble and Rhys in low tones on the other side of the fire, but they stop when I get closer. It feels like I interrupted something.

"What are we talking about?" I say. Peter's eyes have darkened to purple. They *almost* take my breath away.

"Just preparations," Peter says. "How was the trip?"

"I survived."

"I can see that," Peter says with a smile, then turns back to Noble. The way they fell quiet... it's like they don't trust me with whatever they're planning. Peter must still suspect that a copy of Nina resides in me, even though she didn't activate it in the cell.

Sophia is already at the workbench with whatever we picked up at the market. She doesn't look like she wants company, either.

Before I can turn back to the fire, Noble says, "Miranda, I was just telling them about the Torch."

So maybe I'm imagining things.

Now our breath is foggy. Sophia comes over wrapped in a thick shawl, and we all huddle closer to the flames. Rhys hands me a stick with more meat on it, and a small jug of water. I partake of both greedily. He still looks stunned, but I guess catching up with the father you thought was dead will do that to you.

"Where was I?" Noble says.

"Torch," Sophia says.

"Ah, yes. The Torch is an instrument True Earth uses to control the eyeless. The director of True Earth—the Original Miranda—possesses one. A copy was made and then hidden in this world, in case the director's was ever broken or stolen. We cannot let Nina get her hands on it."

"But if we stop Nina, won't the director just come and gather the eyeless herself?" Peter says.

"Yes," Noble replies, "but it will buy us more time. The Torch was hidden here because the eyeless are here. If we can take it from Nina, *we* will control the monsters."

Not something I want to sign up for.

"Do you know where it is?" Rhys asks.

Sophia laughs with her mouth full, like the very idea of knowing the Torch's location is preposterous.

"If I did, I suspect this whole eyeless business wouldn't be much of an issue," Noble says.

Rhys stares into the fire, clearly embarrassed, and I realize I'm waiting for Noah to crack a joke.

"Then how do we find it?" Peter says.

Noble cups his hands and blows into them. "An ally inside the Verge sent me a message. It said, *Tomorrow they ride at dawn for the Torch.* And now so do we."

I climb a few levels to the bathroom, where I'm hoping Noah will appear.

"You're still worried," he says behind me. I turn around. "That Nina is in your head."

"How could you tell?" I regret the sarcasm as I say it.

He laughs and steps closer. "Your mind is like a hurricane. You try to shut your feelings out."

I throw my hands up, and my throat tightens. "She kept me alive, Noah. She took me from the school lab and brought me to some basement, and she didn't kill me."

Noah doesn't speak, just listens.

I was ignoring this part, but now I realize how important it is.

I shouldn't have let Peter convince me to stay.

"And Sequel was able to overpower Nina for a minute, and I asked why, why did she let me live, and she said Nina wanted me for something. So what do you think that is?"

"She didn't change you while you were in the Verge."

I nod and swipe my fingers over my cheeks. "Yeah. That's the only reason I haven't run away."

"And Peter is keeping you at a distance," he says flatly.

"He has to lead," I say.

Noah nods after a moment. "Yeah, he does. Is that who you want to be with? Because that isn't going to change. Pete has always been a leader. Even if he wants you to come first, it goes against everything Tycast and *Sifu* Phil taught him."

I can't deny it. And I'm beginning to understand that our lives might always be this way. I just have to figure out if I can accept it.

"I don't have to lead," Noah says.

"You're—" I stop. What was I going to say? *You're dead*? No. I wouldn't have said that, because he's not dead. This is the first time I allow myself to consider the obvious—with a blank clone and the memory band, he could be here. For real.

"You're right," Noah says. "This is so easy for me too. I love being in here, watching as Peter does the things I used to do." He touches my bottom lip with his thumb. "Those used to be my lips."

"I'm not Sequel," I say. Those were the last lips that belonged to him.

"I know that."

"Just go away so I can pee."

I feel him disappear again, but this time the hole he leaves is a little wider.

We sleep on the cold concrete next to the fire. I wrap myself in a blanket and shiver on the border, where one side of me is too cold, the other too hot. Peter throws his blanket over both of us and pulls me close against his chest. And it's nice.

"Peter..." I say softly. I'm not even sure what I want to say. It's clear he won't be able to fully trust me until this is over.

"I'm sorry I haven't been a good boyfriend," he says.

"We've been busy," I say, but it feels like an automatic response.

"Maybe we can talk about it when this is over."

I don't ask what that means for us in the present. Maybe I should just let him go, let him lead, and worry about what

I'm going to do to keep Nina from taking over my mind and body. Easier said...

Our breathing is off at first—mine is too fast. Then he leans over and kisses me on the corner of my mouth. We don't say a word, but after the kiss our breath syncs and I'm able to fall into a dark and empty sleep.

In the morning there is frost on the floor. The horses exhale long plumes of steam and walk back and forth on the hay. Noble has the fire stoked, and a pot of something oatmealish is bubbling in an honest-to-God cauldron. Sophia and Rhys show up with two new horses, both chestnut brown.

"Used the last of our savings in the market," she says, walking them to the hay.

"We'll get more," Noble says, spooning slop into several bowls. "This'll warm you a bit. Stretch if you can. We need to stay limber for the fighting ahead."

Sophia and Rhys move to the workbench, where she redresses her wound. She won't quite look at him. He keeps trying to put his hands in his pockets, but he's wearing his armor, so it looks like he's just rubbing his thighs weirdly. If I didn't know better, I'd say he's nervous around her.

We eat the tasteless stuff from the cauldron and pass water around. Rhys asks if there's coffee, and Sophia cracks a smile. Even Peter chuckles.

One by one the others stop smiling and remember how dangerous this really is. Sophia shows us to a cabinet full of weapons. Some are in good shape, some not. She and Noble ditched the red gear in favor of something darker. They wear sleeveless charcoal vests and pants that look thick enough to be considered armor. An old gray and curdled scar winds down Noble's left arm.

"I was able to recover your swords," Noble says behind us as we appraise his meager collection. "But your revolvers and ammunition were added to the Red Guard armory. I'm afraid they're lost."

Rhys groans. He loves his gun more than he loves himself. We each take our swords and stick them on our backs. Peter picks a well-maintained shotgun, and Rhys chooses another, smaller sword. I grab the bow and quiver of arrows. The bow luckily has a metal grip, so it sticks to my back, too. The way I see it, the arrows are the only things guaranteed to fire. I don't like to use guns I haven't test-fired and cleaned myself. After we've chosen, Noble gives us wristband radios with little earpieces.

Outside, the sky is still black, but we can see. A light dusting of snow covers the ground, masking the ugliness of everything. Caramel coating on a rotten apple. We could almost be home right now.

Noble walks his horse in front of ours, looking at each of us in turn. "I can't tell you what happens next. And I don't need to tell you what happens if we fail. Strike hard and fast. The worlds are counting on us."

As far as pep talks go, there have been worse.

Together we ride on the gray and white road, back toward the enemy.

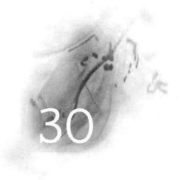

30

I watch as Nina and Gane exit the Verge in my direction.

About five blocks from the Verge, Noble pulled us together to go over our positions. Sophia handed each of us a small steel medallion on a chain, powered by the batteries I picked up with her in the market. In the center of the disk is a red button. "Wear these 'round your necks. If an eyeless comes near you—say, ten feet—press the button. It'll emit a blast of radio waves on every frequency. Enough to cause some interference with their psychic vision."

Ten feet. So, basically, use it if you're about to get eaten.

"Let me guess," Rhys said, turning the medallion over in his fingers. "It won't last long, or only has a few charges."

"The batteries will last, but each radio burst will become

less effective as they adapt. You can use it maybe once or twice."

"Better than nothing," Peter said, at the same time I was thinking it.

"That's one or two charges total, for all of us," Sophia added. "So call it out if you use one."

It's better than nothing, but barely.

Then we split up and picked our way through the streets to cover all the possible exits.

I'm north of the Verge. Rhys and Peter watch from the south and east, respectively, while Noble and Sophia watch from the west, the most likely direction Nina and Gane would head. Instead of the Lincoln Tunnel from our world, Noble told us of a bridge in the same general area, the Lincoln Bridge.

From the shadows inside the Verge's north tunnel, Nina and Gane ride out on two horses. My heart starts to pound. The street used to be Broadway, according to a sign I passed on the way here.

I lift my wrist to my lips and whisper, "I see them. They're moving slowly. What do you want me to do?"

"What direction are they heading?" Noble says in my earpiece.

"Straight north. Straight for me."

Noble sighs. "Okay, they could still turn west for the bridge. Can you move?"

I'm hiding in the doorway of a hollowed-out drugstore. Axela stands quietly just behind me. There's no way to exit without crossing their field of vision; the rear doors are rusted shut.

"Can't make it," I say to my wrist.

Sophia chimes in with, "There's no logical reason for them to go that way."

"Well, they are."

"Hold up," Peter says. "We're behind them."

My chest tightens. Even with the others in pursuit, Nina and Gane will pass very close to me. I poke my head out the door again and see they're only a short block away. Axela snorts and takes a step backward. I cross the room to her, into deeper shadow. It was stupid to corner myself like this.

"Quiet, girl," I whisper to Axela, stroking her mane and scratching under her chin. Her eye gleams in the darkness, and her nostrils flare. "Don't move."

Eight hooves clop on the road outside. My eyes stay on the open doorway for another ten seconds until Gane and Nina come into view, just forty feet away.

They stop outside the doorway.

I hold my breath.

"Do you feel that?" Gane says. He's wearing the same gear as yesterday, but with a long black riding cloak that flows over his horse. Axela sighs through her nose, stirring my hair. Nina is looking right at me, but she doesn't see through the darkness.

"What's happening?" Rhys says in my ear.

"What is it?" Nina says in the street.

But Gane is already walking again. "Nothing," he says. "A feeling." Like he felt my presence, but couldn't be sure.

Nina waits a moment, then follows.

I pat Axela on the shoulder with a shaking hand and whisper, "Good girl." She nuzzles my palm.

Nina and Gane are a full block north when I creep to the doorway. I can't follow them on Axela, but on foot I'm nearly silent. I touch the sword and bow on my back to make sure they're secure, then step into the street, watching for puddles of melted snow.

"Stay back," I whisper to my wrist. "Or come up a different avenue. They're moving too slowly."

I follow them for three more blocks, flitting from doorway to doorway, ducking behind the rusted hulks of vehicles. Holding my breath and praying they don't hear/see/feel me. But this is what I was made for. I see every rock I might disturb, every depression that might trip me up.

Nina and Gane ride side by side, stiff-backed. If they are speaking, it's too quiet for me to hear.

Finally, after another slow block, I see why they came north. Parked on a street corner, right out in the open, is a dirty but intact vehicle I recognize. I saw dozens of them on the streets of Cleveland a few months back. It's an armored Humvee in faded camouflage on huge knobby tires. A Red Guard stands next to it, masked.

"They have a Humvee," I say, feeling like I've been punched in the stomach.

The truck, assuming it works—and why wouldn't it if they came all the way out here?—will allow them to travel faster and farther than us. It won't get tired like our horses.

"Impossible," Noble says.

"I'm looking right at it."

Nina and Gane dismount, and the Red Guard takes the reins of both horses. Nina gets in the driver's seat. The big diesel engine turns over a few times before grumbling to life. A cloud of oily smoke rises from the back. Nina drives it west, presumably toward the Lincoln Bridge. In a few seconds it's gone, hidden behind the next block of buildings.

I turn to run for Axela, but she already came out to follow the other horses. The group canters toward me, and I meet them halfway, pausing to jump onto Axela's back.

"West?" Noble says as I spur my horse forward.

"West," I repeat.

The Humvee isn't the most subtle thing on the planet. It's so loud we could follow it by sound alone, but the giant plume of dust it kicks up is all we need. They take the huge suspension bridge that doesn't exist in our world. The bridge is decrepit, with cables hanging loose and swaying in the wind.

After the bridge, the cities are gone. There is no New Jersey, just flat black ground for miles, as though some enormous bulldozer just came and swept everything away. It hits me that I'm really riding a horse across a dead and empty land, trying to stop my clone from destroying the world.

An hour later, the land doesn't stay flat. It begins to slope upward into a hilly area. The path curls left and right around rocks and boulders the same color as the sky. We approach a bus on its side, rusted and gutted from the bottom, slightly buried, like a long rusty cave.

When we get closer, the back becomes visible. It says SCHOOL BUS, then STOP, then STATE LAW. The bones inside look too small.

No one speaks. We gallop on. The horses wheeze and foam at the mouth, but we only slow enough to keep them alive. I pat Axela from time to time and whisper *sorry*. The horses don't complain, almost like they know where they're taking us and why.

When the school bus is a yellow speck on the horizon, I hear a voice inside my head. It's not Noah's.

"Miranda..." it says.

I can feel my pulse. I look at the others, but their faces are forward.

"Let me out! Let me out! LET ME OUT!" it screams.

I close my eyes and shake my head, ears ringing. *No, no no no.*

Peter is suddenly to my right. "What's wrong? Miranda, what's wrong?"

Everyone is staring.

I know that voice.

"I heard Nina's voice," I whisper to him. My eyes ache with tears I won't let fall. "I shouldn't be here."

"Are you sure?"

"*Yes.*"

For a moment, Peter looks at his hand holding the mane of his horse. I know how torn he is. I should run.

"We need you," he whispers back. "There's nowhere for you to go out here. You can't give her control. Do you hear me?"

I nod, waiting for her to return, but she's quiet. I'm still me.

Ten minutes later the hard ground softens to sand. The crumbling earth changes from gray-black to a dark blue hue. The horses struggle up a hill slowly, footing uneven, then slide down the other side. The dust plume from the Humvee is gone, but the sand holds the deep tread marks well. The tracks guide us like paint in the road.

"Stay ready," Noble says. "These hills are infested."

"With?" Rhys says.

"Guess," Sophia says.

My fingers brush the medallion on my chest, then grasp the bow on my back. I pull it off, lay it across my lap, nock an arrow, and keep my fingers on it, ready to pull back in an instant. My fingertips are sweaty inside my gloves, but the tiny scales keep my grip sure.

We crest another hill and reach flat land again except for directly in front of us, where the ground has split apart in a wide fissure. From space it must look like a deep, ragged cut in bluish skin. We coax our horses closer. The sandy ground is ripped up with claw marks—eyeless claws, wide and deep. Peter's stallion tosses his head around and snorts. Rhys's stops altogether until he kicks a few times. Smart horses.

"There," Noble says.

The Humvee is parked at the bottom of the chasm, in the narrow strip of land where the two walls meet. Nina and Gane are crouched next to it, studying something in the dirt. Seeing Nina makes my heart thrum. Adrenaline burns away my aches.

Nina keeps watch while Gane stands up and holds his arms out, facing away from us. The ground churns at his feet and begins to break apart and flow into a pile on his left. He's digging a hole with his *mind*. The sight chills the sweat on my skin. He can lift a horse. He can root us in place. It's possible he could lift the Humvee and throw it at us before we had a chance to fight.

Only one way to discover his limitations.

"They'll see us if we descend on horses," Sophia says. There's a winding road cut into the valley on the right.

"We move on foot from here," Noble says. "Gane can't control all of us at once. Or if he does, his hold will be weak. His ability comes from a power pack under his armor, wired through his whole nervous system, and it'll be hot from digging the hole. *Don't* try destroying it—the pack is indestructible." So that's the bump I saw under his vest earlier, when he was walking me to the cells.

Over his shoulder, Noble asks the three Roses, "Can you three handle the girl?"

"No question," Rhys says.

Peter nods, but his eyes go to me.

"Miranda?" Noble says.

"Yes," I say. I can handle her as long as I stay myself.

The valley walls are dotted with dark openings in the rock—caves. A narrow white form passes just behind one of the cave openings, half hidden in the gloom.

Noble was right; this place is infested.

"They'll overwhelm us," I say.

Axela shifts her weight and tosses her head. Sitting here makes me want to scream. I have to move and fight to clear my mind.

Noble frowns. "No, I don't think so. The eyeless are watching. They want to see who gets the Torch. If they do come, use your medallions. Get the Torch at any cost, but make sure you can escape with it."

"What happens when one of us gets the Torch?" Rhys says.

"Try to use it," Noble says, dropping a hand on Rhys's shoulder.

"This is suicide." I'm surprised it's Sophia who says it. She gazes over the valley like the rest of us and shakes her head slowly. "This is suicide, Rhys."

At first I think she's talking to my Rhys. I'd feel better if Sophia weren't afraid. Maybe it's not true, but I feel like she has a better idea of the risk. She grew up here, since birth.

Noble climbs off his horse. "It doesn't have to be. We get the Torch, we survive. Very simple." He pulls out a sword of his own, a scimitar. "If any of you can't pull your weight in battle, I ask that you leave now, before endangering the rest of us."

Peter and Rhys almost physically puff themselves up. None of Alpha team would back down, ever.

Except that I nearly leave right then, getting as far as pulling my reins to the left to turn Axela around. But I don't. I just have to stay out of earshot, or, if I can't, block out anything Nina says.

"All right, then," Noble says.

In the distance, Gane has created a pile of dirt taller than the Humvee.

Noble begins to pick his way down the valley wall. The way is steep, but there are countless handholds and platforms to break on. Or break ourselves on, should one of us slip.

"Quickly!" Noble says as we climb off our mounts and follow.

Nina sees us before we're ten feet down the wall. I pause and loose an arrow into the valley. It arcs up and then down and lands three feet from Nina's foot. I fire another one, aiming based on the first arrow's flight, and she watches it arc toward her, then calmly takes a step to the left. The arrow shatters on the rock she was standing on. Her laughter reaches my ears.

Gane considers us for a moment, then jumps into the hole, his riding cloak billowing like a parachute. The dirt flies out in a fury now, almost misting in the air, a bluish geyser.

We descend faster. The rocks blur past as I sprint down the mountain, leaping from clearing to clearing. I bend my knees to absorb the impacts, rolling when I have to. My heart races in a good way, and the fear is pushed into a corner of my mind, because all I focus on is the descent. The others become vague blurry shapes, jumping and scrabbling for traction in my peripheral vision. The buzz of dirt bursting from the hole is thunder to the silent lightning overhead. A shelf of rock collapses under me, and I slide the last ten feet on my heels.

The five of us hit the valley floor at the same time.

"Gane!" Nina shouts. The word echoes off the valley walls.

Gane is still in the hole, but that doesn't stop him from breaking apart the enormous pile of dirt and throwing it at us. The mini-mountain rumbles and disintegrates, and chunks of dirt and rocks zip toward us in a moving desert storm. I duck and press my forearm to my eyes as the stinging grit hits me full in the face. Rocks ping off my armor. I hear a wet *thunk*, and Rhys groans next to me. I hear Peter fall to his knees, but I can't open my eyes yet. The wind and debris hammers us until my hair is heavy with dirt and my eyes are too caked to open.

"Rhys! Peter!" I say, and get a mouthful of dirt as a reward.

"Fine," Peter yells over the roar. "I'm fine!"

Finally the wind stops.

The air is foggy with bluish dirt. A breeze pumps through the valley and clears the air some.

I blink the gunk out of my eyes and see the one thing we came to prevent.

Tears of frustration turn the dirt in my eyes to mud. Sheer stubbornness keeps my knees from collapsing. We came all this way to be stopped by a pile of dirt. Our world is lost because of a dirt pile.

The others stand up around me and dust themselves off, making small sounds in their throats when they see what I see.

Nina holds the Torch high above her head.

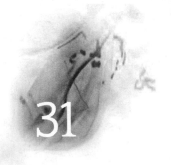

31

I have no thought besides *She must die*. As Gane pulls himself out of the hole, I run toward Nina, then skid to a stop thirty feet away, feet churning up the loose dirt. The Torch earned its name. It's a staff of shining metal nearly four feet tall. The end is capped by a glowing ball of red light too bright to look at. I focus on Nina's face instead.

I pull an arrow from my quiver, then string it and pull back in the same motion. The whole movement takes a half second. Nina hasn't even begun to move yet, save for a slight widening of her eyes. I see only her; her hand tightens on the Torch, but if she was planning to bring the eyeless down to stop me, they're too far away, still hidden in their caves. The arrow zips through the air, straight for Nina's face.

Until Gane waves his hand like he's swatting a gnat, and the arrow curves up and tumbles harmlessly behind them, past the Humvee puffing oily smoke into the air.

Nina smiles, and the Torch glows brighter, a stoked coal. The eyeless surface in unison and huddle in the dark openings. Thousands of white, eyeless heads cluster in the caves, all the way up the walls. I fight to keep my eyes on the threat in front of me, not the threat waiting for me. But the sight of them does what Nina probably intended—it shakes us. Someone gasps behind me. Rhys mutters a curse.

Ending this is the only thing that will save us. My fingers are deft and sure, even if my mind is not. I grab for another arrow, but Gane's eyes are on me now, and I feel his mind too. He tears the quiver from my back and the leather rips into pieces and the arrows all tumble out, floating around me, spiraling, until they explode into a cloud of sawdust the wind carries away as soon as it's formed. Splinters stab at the exposed skin on my face. I squint against them, going to one knee as Gane forces me to kneel. Behind me, I hear the others hitting the ground. He can't control all of us at once, Noble said. I can only marvel at how resolve can melt into despair this fast. I want to move, and charge, and fight, but I can't. I keep waiting for the eyeless to pour down from the walls and cover us like a blanket.

But wait. The hold on me is tenuous. I feel Gane's mind

ebbing on my skin, barely keeping all of us in place. I have to wait for the right moment. I can still do this. I can save us.

"Give me the Torch," Gane says to Nina, holding out his hand. When she hesitates for a second, Gane tries to rip it from her hands with his mind. But Nina's grip is strong.

The Torch flies toward Gane with Nina still attached. He tries to duck, but her fist slams into his temple. She lands on her feet.

Gane's mouth opens, eyes rolling back in his head, and the hold on me disappears completely. He falls to his knees in the dirt, sagging, and Nina swings the Torch like a golf club. Gane flinches away, but it catches the top of his head and knocks him on his back. He writhes in the dirt, stirring it with his heels.

I stand up and hear the others do the same behind me. We're thirty feet away, but close enough to rush Nina.

She is heaving, breathless. "Come at me and I'll bring them down on all of us!"

I want to say she's bluffing, but I don't know how the Torch works. I have to trust that Nina didn't come all this way just to sacrifice herself.

I do a quick mental rundown of our weapons. Peter is the only one with a gun, but it's a shotgun. Firing it would risk destroying the Torch, which could have consequences I don't want to think about.

But Peter must not care.

220

He steps up beside me and hefts the shotgun to his shoulder. He's willing to take that risk.

Nina's eyes are different. They're wide, but not with surprise. It's like she's seeing something only in her mind. It must be distracting, because she doesn't even try to move. Peter's shotgun booms, and the armor over Nina's legs sparks and she sprawls face-first in the dirt. I almost scream in triumph. The shot didn't seem to breach her armor, but she's down, and that's a step in the right direction.

The Torch rolls away from her open fingers, and she squirms just like Gane did.

Gane, who is suddenly no longer on the ground. I don't see him anywhere.

The important thing is Nina let go of the Torch, but it doesn't have the effect I was hoping for. The eyeless are no longer hiding inside the dark of their caves.

Thousands of them are descending with a unified scream.

32

They converge on us from both sides, twin waves of white pouring down the valley walls. I force myself to look away. If I don't, I'll freeze. They'll wash over me and turn my body into red mist.

Instead I focus on what we came for.

I sprint for the Torch as Nina rolls onto her back and chokes on a scream. A guttural sound half pain and half rage. The sandy dirt rises off the ground and swirls around us, but I can't tell if it's Gane or just the wind. My eyes sting but I keep moving. The distance is only thirty feet, but it feels like the Torch is a mile away. I can hear the eyeless coming closer; the scraping of thousands of claws on rock blur into a buzz.

Nina grabs for the staff and falls short, fingers clawing in the dirt. I'm ten feet away now. She gets up on one elbow and lunges again, but I skid to a stop and pick up the Torch as Nina clamps her hand on the staff, next to mine.

The Torch vibrates under my grip. Power rolls up my arm and into my brain, and I get a glimpse of everything around me, filtered through a thousand psychic minds, all connected. It's breathtaking and overwhelming, but at the same time completely natural. I see with their minds, I see *us*, as they barrel down the walls, claws reaching forward, gripping rock. I see with their minds as Peter tracks the leading one with his shotgun. I see Gane staggering away from the group, holding his head with both hands. I see Rhys sidestep an eyeless and knock it into the huge hole with his dual swords, only to be pulled in when the already dying monster catches his ankle. Vaguely I'm aware that Rhys can handle one eyeless, but that his absence will hurt us.

Then they're on us, and I force the vision away.

Nina has enough time to pull herself up while I blink rapidly, disoriented as my normal vision returns. It was too much too fast, enough of an opening for her to rip the Torch from my hand. The eyeless *stop*. I feel normal instantly, never wanting to touch the thing again, and realizing I absolutely have to.

The closest eyeless is only ten feet away, swelling and shrinking with each breath, claws half buried in the dirt. It's coiled up to launch at me. The milky skin is almost translucent, showing the sharp tendons and muscle fibers underneath. Right before it leaps, I slap the medallion on my chest and the eyeless rears up and spins around, confused and unsteady, suddenly drunk.

"One charge!" I shout. One or two left, if we're lucky.

I make another grab for the Torch, even get my fingers on it, but Nina snaps her head forward and head-butts me full in the face. My feet leave the ground and my vision fuzzes, and warm blood pours from my nose and over my lips.

I hit the dirt and the pain disappears. The lights go out.

And reappear the next second. The word *No* is on my mind. She can't have it. Someone needs to step in and take it. I blink and sit up, gritting my teeth against the throb in my face and body. The eyeless flow away from us in a stampede, heading back in the direction we came.

Back toward the city and the Black. They ignore us now. In a few minutes they'll be gone and we'll be stuck here, miles and miles from anything. This can't be it. This is supposed to end another way.

My vision clears in time to see Nina getting into the Humvee with the Torch. I stand up only to get bowled over by an eyeless trying to catch up with its pack. It's like being tackled by a five-foot-tall spider. I hear a *ting* and see two of the scales on my suit pop off and fly away, victims of eyeless claws. Then it's gone, galloping with the others. It happens so fast I don't have time to be afraid, barely enough time to get an arm in front of my throbbing face.

The Humvee is already tearing toward the winding road on the valley wall. I spare a look for the others.

Sophia and Gane are missing. Peter is helping Rhys out of the hole, back turned. Good. I don't want to say good-bye, or hear his protests. Noble stands over the hacked corpse of an eyeless, blood dripping off his chin.

In the distance, the Humvee reaches the bottom of the road and begins the long climb.

I sprint toward the wall we first descended, leaving the others in the center of the valley. All that matters is stopping Nina. Our world depends on it.

I try to judge if I can make it to the top of the valley before her, but it's too close to tell. The road curves back and forth up the wall maybe twelve times, close to a quarter mile on each straightaway, followed by a hairpin turn that sends Nina back the other way. While I have to climb in a straight line.

"Suck it up, Miranda," Noah says.

Normally that would annoy me. He's been gone for the hard parts but returns with sage advice.

I ignore him, but he's right.

I suck it up and climb.

❀   ❀   ❀

I don't see the eyeless until I'm on top of it. It springs out from behind a rock, and for a second I think I'm dead. I'm near the top of the valley wall with no place to run. This thing stayed behind and now it's going to kill me. But its lower half is shattered, victim to the stampede. It has to drag its legs along like dead weight. The claws work fine, though. They swipe at my throat from above and tear more scales from my armor, shredding the chain holding my medallion. My balance is gone. I grab for a handhold but touch air, and then I'm falling from hundreds of feet up.

Thinking, *What a terrible way to die.*

The wind howls louder as I pick up speed. Noah doesn't speak, but his fear floods my mind. He gives me his, and I give him mine, and, in a way, we hold each other.

There are worse ways to die.

I shut my eyes and wonder if I have a soul.

33

Instead of dropping faster, I begin to slow.

The wind isn't rushing in my ears; gentle hands seem to break my fall, but I don't open my eyes, not yet.

Not until I stop.

In midair, halfway down the valley wall. The feeling on my skin is familiar. At the top of the wall, Gane floats a few feet in front of the edge, arm out and palm down, like I'm a marionette a hundred feet below him.

Slowly, I begin to rise.

"That was fun," Noah says.

Oh my God, is all I can reply.

Gane probably didn't save me because he likes me. The way he's floating now, I assume he levitated up the side of the valley to stop Nina, since the Humvee will come out right there at the top. The wound on his head bleeds down his face. His eyes hold not anger, but determination.

"Miranda!" Peter shouts below me.

I twist my head around as my ascent quickens. Peter and Rhys stand at the base of the wall I'm floating up. Noble and Sophia hobble along behind them, helping each other stay upright. The Humvee is nearly to the top now, careening around a dusty turn at the far end, the diesel engine filling the valley with its clatter. It'll pass by so close. *Be ready,* I think. *Fling her off the road.* I want it so badly.

I reach the top, and Gane sets me down lightly near the edge. His black hair is thick with dirt and dripping sweat. I can feel the heat pouring off the power pack under his vest. Behind him, our horses haven't fled from the eyeless exodus. Looking closer, I can tell it's because Gane has them rooted in place. They're rigid, but with terrified eyes, white and rolling. They're itching to escape.

"She told me I would have the Torch," he says, grim-faced. "I didn't believe her, but I thought I could *take it.*"

I dust myself off and check for broken bones. I squeeze my nose with my thumb and forefinger; it aches, but seems whole. "What other lies did she tell you?" I say.

"That she would take them to one of the empty worlds. To banish them."

"Did you believe her? Do you?"

His gaze falls, and he clenches his jaw. "No. But if I had the Torch I knew I could do it myself."

"Then *help me*. Help me stop her."

He nods. "But what of the eyeless?"

"Once I gain control of the Torch, I promise to take them to one of the empty worlds."

The Humvee is getting closer.

"I won't be betrayed twice. When we get to her, *I* wield the Torch."

"Where else would I want to take them? I'm fighting *her*."

"I don't care."

Not like I have a choice. And I believe Gane. He wouldn't have saved me otherwise.

Nina rounds the last bend, heading right for us, rising all the while.

"Do you agree?" he says without looking at me.

"Yes."

She's a few hundred feet away now. The engine screams, amplified by the valley wall next to it.

"I have a favor. One favor." With Gane in one piece and fully aware this time, we can take care of Nina. So I need to protect the others, even if they'll hate me for it.

"What is it?" he says.

"If she gets past us, keep the others from following. We can handle this alone." I appeal to his hubris. "It's just one girl, two of us, and you know who the enemy is now."

"Fine."

The Humvee skids around a huge boulder in the path, kicking up rooster tails of dirt and sand. Gane reaches out with both hands and the front wheels come off the ground, then slam back down. The Humvee turns sideways even though the wheels are still pointed straight.

"Too heavy!" he gasps. "Too fast!" Gane's last attempt is to throw it over the side; the outer wheels scrabble at the edge, but Nina jerks the wheel and keeps it on the road. I catch a glimpse of her in the driver's seat, one hand on the wheel and one on the Torch. She blows past us in a roar of dust and hot exhaust.

Axela twitches under me when I jump on. "Release us!" I tell Gane.

He does, and Axela almost bucks me off. She spins in a circle, hooves stamping the ground. "Easy, girl, easy!" I pat her flank and she calms, just slightly.

"You coming?" I point to the nearest horse.

Gane climbs on, and, true to his word, he releases the other horses. Axela and I almost get plowed over as they take off in a panicked stampede. Gane keeps his horse under control. It's a long walk back to the Verge for the others, but a small price to pay for their safety.

Nina's Humvee is on flat ground now, past where the hills

end. Beyond her, I see a moving white blanket on the horizon—thousands of eyeless at her command. Something catches my eye to the north—another blanket, just as large. To the south is another, larger yet. There have to be tens of thousands of eyeless, all of them responding to the Torch's call.

Peter and Rhys yell my name as they climb.

I sag on Axela, gripping her mane to stay upright. My energy seeps out of me. Nina is already so far away, with her army laid out before us. No matter what, her head start will cost lives.

"The Torch is everything," Gane says. "Survive long enough to take it."

I ditch the pity party; we're still alive. It's not over.

I snap the reins, and Axela takes off after the monsters.

We have to stop a mile from the city to let the eyeless horde pass. It's either stop or ride into them. They pour in from all directions, from all corners of the Blasted Lands, Gane says. I assume they've been given the order to head to the Black, but I'm not going to test if they're allowed to stop and kill us. They keep coming.

And coming.

And coming.

They ignore us, thankfully. It's clear Nina holds them in thrall, commanding them to the same place.

"How many?" I ask.

Gane can only shake his head. "They've been multiplying for years. It took far fewer than this to bring my world to its knees."

Any strength I've managed to gather dissolves. If a world that was once as mighty as Gane's could fall to less, how long will our world be able to stand? There won't even be a fight. Suddenly I regret stranding the others back in the valley. I need them. I need them to hold me up. And I can't ignore the shame I feel—I made the choice for them. If someone told me I couldn't fight...just to keep me safe...

That's exactly what Noah did to me, when he stole my memories. And it only made things worse.

We sit in silence while the horde continues to funnel into the city. I check behind me, but the others are nowhere in sight.

"They'll go to the Verge," Gane says. "The Black in Central Park is sealed."

I say nothing.

When the horde passes, we canter into the city on its tail, coughing on the massive grimy cloud it churned up. A few stragglers limp along the Lincoln Bridge, deformed or injured eyeless not strong enough to keep up. As we pass, Gane tears them apart with his mind. I try to judge how vast his powers are in case we somehow fight again in the future. He can't stop the horde, but he can destroy a few eyeless here and there. And a Humvee is obviously too heavy for him to control.

I block out the noise of shredding flesh and dying wails, keeping my eyes on the Verge as it steadily grows larger. With each eyeless Gane kills, I almost feel happy; it's one more that won't join the assault on my world. The streets are empty, but signs of the passing horde are everywhere. Rusted but intact vehicles are now crumpled, as if victims of a hailstorm, with huge dimples in the hoods and roofs. Then we're at the Verge, still riding hard. I charge into the dark tunnel the way Noah charged into the dark room, waiting for a sword to take my neck or an eyeless to yank me off Axela and into the shadows.

The torches are on the ground, some extinguished, some smoldering. Gane pounds next to me until we reach the tunnel's end, where we have to stop so fast I almost fly over Axela's head. The main floor of the Verge is gone—completely gone. *All* of it. The other tunnel entrances end in open air too, traps for whoever charges down the tunnel blindly like we did. The destruction of a solid place where I once stood makes my skin tingle.

Hundreds of feet down, a narrow walkway is attached to the rock walls in the shape of a ring. The walkway is only a few feet wide. The rest of the floor is a bottomless black hole. Pure nothingness, empty and still. It's my first time seeing the

Black in person since finding out what it is. I have to swallow several times to keep from throwing up. The vertigo only fades when I close my eyes.

This is the first time I realize that the end is really here. The eyeless have already gone through. My task is nearly impossible. I have to travel through the Black and survive long enough to find Nina. That's it. I have to survive long enough to beat her. Survive long enough to save the world. But even then, I don't know where I'll take them. I don't know where to take thousands of monsters.

"End of the line, girl," Gane says.

"You aren't coming with?" I almost laugh.

"My place is here. We didn't make it in time. I am sorry for your world, but I am beholden to my people. The Torch is gone."

"It isn't," I say, a simple denial that sounds childish.

Gane shakes his head. "I could've prevented this."

"But you didn't, because you're a fool." Gane doesn't reply, instead staring down into hell with me. I want to tear his head off for making this possible, but it won't change a thing. It won't make me feel better, or give me hope.

Gane grabs my arm and digs his fingers in. "If you can get the Torch, bring the eyeless back here. Pack them into the Verge. I will take my people away. In my office are enough explosives to destroy this place. You'll kill the eyeless and seal the Black." He tells me the passwords to get into his office and where to find the explosives.

He doesn't tell me how to get out after setting them off.

"Go now," he says.

I take a breath and kick my heels into Axela, hoping she'll jump. If Nina is on foot, maybe I can use her to catch up. And being atop her makes me feel safer, even if I'm not.

But she doesn't budge, just snorts through her nose and flicks her tail.

"Give me a push?"

Gane nods and raises his hands. Axela comes off the ground, then bolts forward as soon as her hooves touch rock. We leap out into open air, and gravity pulls us toward the Black. The hole grows bigger and bigger in my vision until it's all I can see.

I close my eyes.

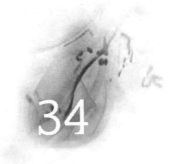

34

I open my eyes to the huge cavern we first came through, with all the tunnels leading to different cities. The lake of Black is to my left, a perfect circle two feet away. My wounds throb anew. My stomach gurgles, and I roll over and spew black oil for the second time in two days. Some of my hair falls past my face, still auburn.

Axela has black liquid dripping from her mouth too. I push myself up slowly and blink away the disorientation. The cavern is filled with the tangled and twisted metal from the Verge's main floor. Nina must've somehow collapsed the floor into the Black, which then vomited it up into the cavern, like it did with me.

The stone floor is covered in claw marks.

I realize I still hoped the Black led somewhere else, that I would open my eyes to a different world. Now even that hope is gone.

The gouges in the stone all lead in one direction—to the tunnel labeled WASHINGTON, D.C. That particular tunnel entrance is thick with the same gouges, while the other openings are pristine. It all makes sense now. After removing our government, the eyeless will come back and disperse through the tunnels to different parts of the country, and then around the globe.

I reach back and feel Beacon, my sword, but I lost the bow somewhere along the way, which doesn't really matter since Gane decided to explode all my arrows. Nothing left to do here but swing my leg over Axela and ride down the tunnel.

The trip takes no time at all, less than five minutes of hard riding, which means the cavern must sit directly under D.C. This was the plan all along, the plan for *decades*. I keep my ears tuned for sounds of the eyeless, but everything is quiet. The tunnel begins to slope up. We're nearing the end, I can feel it, and the adrenaline is welcome. I find myself straightening on Axela's back, eager to get above ground. The world may be ending, but it isn't over. "C'mon girl," I say, urging her along. The tunnel continues its upward slope until I see stars in a black sky—*my* sky—and then we're up and out, hooves

237

thumping on grass in cool night air that tastes clean and fresh and just like home.

Artificial light illuminates the ground in front of me, and I turn Axela around with my left heel.

We're next to the Washington Monument.

Right in front of me is a pile of shredded clothes covered in blood. A tennis shoe pokes out. At the base of the monument is another eviscerated pile of clothes and stuff that is not clothes, all of it red. Screams rise in the distance, layering over one another, rising, rising. I turn in a slow circle, looking for signs of life, but expecting to see none this close to the ramp. And I'm right. Axela snorts and tosses her head from side to side, thoroughly freaked at the smell of blood. "Easy, girl, easy," I say, patting her flank, for as much my benefit as hers.

The screams are loudest to the north, where I can see the tiny back of the White House surrounded by trees glowing with bright lights. If they're going to wipe out our government, I can't think of a better place to start. Nina might be there, in the center of everything. I spur Axela onward until she's in a full gallop toward the White House.

Gunfire rattles in the night. A siren blares, like the kind in old war movies. Sirens from emergency vehicles mix in with the nightmare sounds.

After the monument is a wide street of six lanes, then more grass before the White House's south lawn. Ahead is a collapsed fence, as if the eyeless decided it was easier to knock it down than leap over it. More gunfire crackles in the distance, like fireworks. I imagine the confusion. People don't know what's coming for them, or why.

The Secret Service knows, but can't possibly understand. A hundred yards away, they burst out of the White House in dark suits. Bright white spotlights light the agents from behind, while a cluster of eyeless approach from darkness. It's just a group of fifteen to twenty of the monsters, a pack. There's only time for a few bursts of automatic gunfire—Axela suddenly sidesteps behind a copse of trees, tossing her head, and I struggle to move her forward. The gun muzzles flash with orange light, and then the eyeless overtake them. Clothes shred and blood sprays and I feel empty because the men never had a chance. It happened so fast, there probably wasn't time for much fear or pain. Axela pounds the ground, moving under me, but she isn't quick enough. And it wouldn't matter anyway, because I don't mean to face the eyeless, not like this. Even if I could fight that many at once, what would it do? Nothing. The Torch is the key. It becomes a mantra in my mind. Finding Nina is the key. She has to be here. Why else would the eyeless be swarming in this direction?

The eyeless funnel through the doors into the executive residence of the White House, no longer silent but screaming. The screams are of delight and hunger, so different from the screams of the dying.

I'm twenty yards away when the last eyeless slips inside. An agent groans on his back in the Rose Garden to the left. He lifts a bloody hand like he's waving to the sky. I stop Axela next to the agent and jump off. She spins away from me, and for a second I fear she's going to bolt, but she just prances in a circle, eyeing the space around us.

The agent's suit is torn open. Where his stomach is supposed to be is a blood-filled hole the size of my fist. Blood pumps out in time with his heart, soaking the grass. This man is dying here because of the place I came from.

His eyes widen in fear when he sees me. "You . . ." he croaks. He recognizes me.

"I'm not her. Listen, I'm not the same girl. I'm not her. Where is she? Have you seen her?" I kneel and grip his shoulders lightly, then snap my head up at a noise from inside the White House. It sounded like a watermelon being dropped on concrete from ten feet.

The agent's eyes keep rolling up. I need to know.

"Hey, you can help stop this. Tell me where she is." *Please know something. Please.*

His lips make an O-shape.

"Where? Where?" I lay my hand along his cheek. "It's okay. Tell me. I can stop this." Maybe if I say it enough, it'll be true.

"Oval..."

The Oval Office.

"Where? Where?" I try to remember my history lesson on this place, but it's fuzzy. The agent tilts his head and moves his eyes to his right. The Oval Office kind of bulges off the West Wing, with vertical windows taller than I am. Windows that are just openings now, the glass blown out.

Two Humvees roar behind me and turn onto the lawn, big knobby tires digging into the grass. They skid to a stop outside the East Wing. Soldiers pile out and ready assault weapons. They're too far away for me to get their attention, but I try anyway. "Wait, stop! Stop!" My voice is drowned out by the scream of a jet overhead. The soldiers fast-march into the building, doomed. When I look back down, the agent is still, eyes unseeing. The lack of light in his eyes reminds me of Noah and makes me wish he were here. It reminds me this could be my last minute as myself. When I go into the Oval Office, Nina might kill me—or worse, erase me. But I'm ready for whatever comes next.

"You're not alone."

Noah's sudden words give me strength.

I pull Beacon off my back and sprint the hundred feet to the Oval Office, slowing just before I reach it. Thick red light spills out from the window frames, dappling the grass with blood.

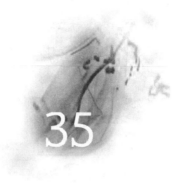

35

I take one step, then another, leading the way with Beacon's tip. Finally I reach the window frame and step through. The Torch lights the room a brilliant red. Nina sits behind the president's desk, hunched forward and still. Seeing her so close, with her back to me, I almost freeze in surprise. But the hesitation fades in the next second, and I swing Beacon in a horizontal slash, intending to take her head and end the fight before it begins, knowing it means I won't get answers from her; I won't be able to shake her and ask why.

Nina dips her torso to the left like she's stretching, and the blade whistles over her harmlessly, pulling me off balance. I put so much behind the strike, so sure it would land. She bursts upright and mule-kicks the chair back at me, then rolls forward over the desk. She lands on the other side and spins around with the Torch held in front of her. She's standing directly on the presidential seal, between two plush couches.

I'm already heaving and near breathless. *Sifu* Phil's lesson is like a shout in my ears—*Erase the emotion. A calm mind delivers sure strikes.*

Seconds pass where she's out of reach, but Nina doesn't say the code. I'm still me.

Her right hand holds a straight sword identical to mine, save the black grip tape she's wrapped around the hilt. She grins. The Torch makes it look like she has blood on her teeth. "Why are you fighting me, Miranda? Put down your sword and I'll take you to True Earth. You can join the army of Roses."

Despite the sickening rage in my chest, tears jump to my eyes. "Why are you doing this?" I guess I get to ask her after all.

"Because this world is like the one we just left—*sick*. One day it will reach critical mass and become a cancer that will spread to other worlds. Call it preventative surgery on the collective universe. Call it saving you from yourselves."

That's it, right there. We're just a tumor to them. And I see it too. Maybe our world has more bad than good. We kill one another over stupid things, or we let people die. We are selfish. They aren't wrong in those respects. And maybe the people of my world are too stubborn to change. We might always be this way, until the world destroys itself.

But it's not Nina's call to make. Or anyone else's from True Earth.

"You know I'm right," she says. "Open your eyes."

The time to say the code has passed—I want to believe that. But something is wrong. . . . She doesn't seem worried at all. It's like she really wants me to join her, and knows she'll get her way in the end.

My mind is whirring, but I'm not considering her offer like she thinks.

"You're fighting on the wrong side, Miranda. *We're* the defenders. Help me. It's what you were made to do. Think about it—how different can we really be? We're the same person."

I don't want to think about that. We might be the same, but I've never felt I could be like her, or Mrs. North, or the director. It's your choices that make you who you are.

And I choose to fight.

Nina is giving me one more chance, one more moment to lean toward her cause. And who wouldn't want to join the winning side?

"Choose," she says.

Already did. She can see it on my face now.

"Then I'm sorry. It's time to wake up, Nina. Be free."

A lightning bolt sears my brain, blinding me. I go to one knee, Beacon loose in my grip. I feel the copy of Nina barge into my mind with a victory scream, and I understand in that brief moment that Mrs. North did taint me with a copy of Nina, that she was inside me all along. There is the vague sensation of tears running down my face, and of utter darkness swooping in, pushing me aside, and one thought—*This is really happening*—before a moment of darkness so pure, I'm sure that I'm gone. But then Noah rises up within me, roaring in defiance, and somehow he takes my hand and pulls me out of the ether. In the next instant, I feel our combined power crush Nina into oblivion. She's gone in a single moment. I hear a thought, either mine or Noah's, I can't tell—*No room for three in here.*

I open my eyes.

"Impossible . . ." Nina says.

I'm still on one knee, but that changes when I stand up. Noah's strength courses through me, mingling with my own. Together we're strong enough to beat her.

"Apparently not," I reply.

Her eyes are wide with fear.

I move right, beginning to circle around the desk. "Who are you, really?"

"I am the director's daughter." She seems to be regaining her composure.

"No, you were my friend. I saw you wake up on a table. So how did you get inside my friend?" *Where is she?* I want to scream.

Her lip curls in a sneer. "Your friend is gone. My true body remains in True Earth, but I loaned my identity to a new body for this mission. I spent the last few months seeing your world firsthand, hiding in the back of Sequel's mind, and when the time was right, I put in a request with the DJ."

The violation of having a secret observer in your mind at all times makes my stomach turn.

"Are you ready to finish this?" she says, holding her hands wide in welcome, Torch in the left, sword in the right.

I'm ready.

The desk is still between us. Outside, I hear another jet roar through the sky, and more gunfire. I want to keep her talking. If I have to make her think, she might give me an opening—just a calm second where I can lunge and end the dance before it begins.

I step forward, a feint.

Nina swipes her sword up slowly, vertically, meaning to cut me up the middle. It's lazy. I parry down and across with Beacon and then step back, putting the desk between us again.

I visualize Nina's blood on my blade, the way Noah's coated hers.

Nina charges. She tries to impale me across the desk and I slap her blade down. It gouges into the ancient wood. Papers scatter sideways, seesawing to the floor.

She turns her blade sideways and tries to cut at my thighs, but I jump back, swishing my sword through the open space in front of her.

"Your plan sucks," I say, trying to distract her with words. "You know they secured the president at the first sign of trouble."

"It's a sign," she says, circling the desk. I hold my ground. Every second I waste with her spreads the eyeless infection further. "I'm showing the world something right now. The images alone will soften them up. They'll be ripe with terror." She lets her blade drop to the desk and scrape the surface.

We're both behind the desk now. Nothing between us but air.

Nina slashes the air in a repeating X, forcing me to back-pedal until I parry. Sparks burst, and the hilt wrenches my wrist. I kick out my heel for the inside of her knee, and she goes down on that knee. The rush of victory floods my limbs—with her below me, she's exposed, at my mercy. I just have to lower my blade to her throat.

Then she surprises me; she drops her sword, grabs my

wrists with both hands, quick as snakebites, and falls onto her back, taking me with her. Her foot rises and plants in my stomach as she pulls me down, then lifts me over her head as her fall turns into a roll. She tosses me over her. I'm upside down when I hit the far wall and crumple on the floor, stunned. But the rage builds and gives me clarity.

The air is sweet with roses; Nina is releasing her fear-waves.

I stand up. Beacon is a few feet away, between us, glowing like a ruby in the light of the Torch.

I fit my armored toe under Beacon and kick it up, then pluck it out of the air and spin, slashing horizontally, each spin bringing me closer to Nina. She intercepts the last slash with her own sword, stopping me. The hilt vibrates in my hand. And suddenly we're chest to chest, blades crossed between us, noses inches apart. My left hand cups the back of her neck; hers does the same, pressing the Torch's shaft against the base of my skull. The metal is hot. The red bulb burns bright in the corner of my left eye. We pull with one hand and press with the other. Our blades scrape together. This is the moment. The world is stuck between two scraping blades. Hers is close to my neck. Mine is close to hers.

"Give up," she grunts. "Kneel."

More talking, when the time for talking is over. I snap my head forward and smash my forehead into her nose, returning the head-butt she offered me only hours ago. I feel her nose cave like wet clay, and blood that isn't mine flecks my face. Dizziness washes over me, but I slough it off.

"I owed you one," I say as she stumbles back. But I don't stop there. This person took not one but two of my friends, and they deserve justice. I follow her, slashing out again horizontally. Her neck makes the same sound when my sword bites into it that Noah's did. There's a burst of blood and her back hits the wall.

I see my mistake, but it's too late.

The Torch slips from her fingers, and the red bulb shatters on the floor.

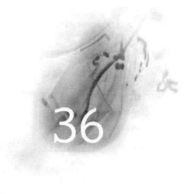

36

The Torch crackles, red electricity dancing over the carpet. Nina slides down the wall, blood flowing out of her neck. She tries to say something, but she can only cough blood onto her lips. I stow Beacon, then snatch up the Torch and hold it with both hands and close my eyes to feel something, *anything*, but it's dead, just a shaft of metal. Dead like Nina is about to be. I watch her eyes dim while I wait for the Torch to turn on, because it can't be broken, not after everything we went through to get it.

If Nina could talk, she'd say, *You still lose*.

Thousands of eyeless scream in the night as they're set free. I fall to my knees.

I failed; the eyeless have no master now. Nothing will stop them from roaming the world. And if Gane is right, they'll never quit. Just keep eating and multiplying until our world is as barren as his.

The gunfire has dropped away to random and faraway drumrolls. I set my forehead against the cool curved wall of the office and close my eyes.

I don't want to feel anymore; I don't want to lose.

"We should kill them," Noah says.

I spin around awkwardly on my knees and almost slip in Nina's blood. Noah stands next to the president's desk, half leaning against it with five fingertips.

"We should kill them all," he says. His face is pure rage. His hands curl into fists. "We should go to True Earth and kill the Originals and anyone who stands with them."

"I don't know what to do."

"We never knew what to do."

I rise, muscles groaning in my back and legs. "They're free now."

An explosion rocks the night. Another jet screams overhead. All of it sounds farther away than before. Like Commander Gane said, the cancer is spreading.

"So we find a way to stop them." He walks to me and uses his finger to lift my chin. "Do you know why I love you?"

"No."

"Because you're strong. You never give up."

"You don't love me." My voice cracks. How much longer do I have to be strong? Not long. It's over, so he should know the truth. He should know before we both die. He should be able to feel something else, something real.

"Why not?" he says.

"Because I'm not really Miranda."

He looks into my eyes. His hands cup my face gently.

Tears run down my cheeks all at once. This is where I stop holding my secret. His thumbs wipe my tears, even though I know that's impossible. "When you left her..." I swallow. "She died. And Mrs. North used me to replace her. The memory fragments I have belong to the girl before me."

I've just killed him again. It's plain on his face.

"Miranda..." he says, shaking his head.

I kiss him.

It isn't right, or even real, but somehow I do it. While the world begins its slow death around us. His lips are soft at first, unsure, but then they react. "I'm sorry," he says with his lips against mine. "I'm sorry."

"You didn't know."

"I always—" he begins.

Just outside, I hear the unmistakable rising whistle of

a fired rocket, then a short, sharp explosion that shakes the walls and wakes us up. Noah takes my hand and squeezes it once.

"The director still has a Torch. Don't you dare give up."

He disappears.

As the Torch begins to rumble behind me.

The bulb doesn't glow; it can't; it's still broken.

But the metal shaft vibrates on the floor next to Nina.

I stare at it for a moment, dumbstruck, watching it dance on the carpet. I pick it up and the vibration tickles my palms. I wait. There's nothing else to do. The vibration has to mean something. Maybe it's a final death rattle, or whatever's inside the shaft trying to turn back on.

Then it stops.

Another rocket whistles nearby, followed by man-made thunder.

The Torch isn't moving, but it *feels* like it wants to get away, like my hands and the Torch just became opposite magnets. A breeze cuts through the office, bringing the mixed scent of pine and hot metal. The room around me begins to darken, like it's fading from existence, and suddenly I can't feel my palms. The Black is spreading around my fingers, over the backs of my hands. A few seconds later it's up my arms, down my legs, across my chest, erasing me bit by bit. The Black crawls up my neck, my chin. Over my face.

I hold on tight and close my eyes, and when I open them, I'm in a different place entirely.

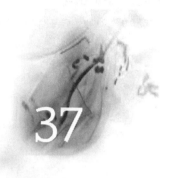

37

I t takes me a second to understand what happened as I fall to my hands and knees, gagging. The Black enveloped me, and now I'm not in the Oval Office, but outside—I feel a sweet breeze and the open sky above me, even though I haven't looked around yet. The urge to vomit is strong and hot, but the feeling passes after a few seconds and a few swallows. I blink and breathe and look at the smooth metal floor under my gloved hands. The Torch begins to roll away from me, and I lunge for it, but it stops under someone's toe.

The toe belongs to a foot covered in armor identical to mine, but with brilliant golden scales instead of black. I've seen those scales before on the director, in Mrs. North's memory. The gold is the same color as the wall to my left; to my right is open air—we're on a walkway attached to the side of a golden building.

I look up, fingers still on the Torch, completely exposed on all fours.

An Olivia stares down at me. She could be my Olive, but she's not.

"Where did you get this?" she says.

I scan her body language in an instant—she's relaxed. Her narrowed eyes study me; not surprised to see me, but more... impressed. I'm not a threat.

Her eyes flick down to the Torch. "You broke it."

"No I didn't," I say before I can stop myself. Behind her the sky is golden, like that time near sunset before all the reds appear. Yet the *entire* sky glows gold, when it should be one end or the other. Which leads me to believe this isn't my sky at all. I see tall buildings from the corner of my right eye, but I don't dare take my eyes off the girl, no matter how much I want to look.

"Get up," she says, reaching down. I swing at her purely out of reflex, and she bats my hand away lightning fast, no more effort than I would need to block a child. "Don't do that again."

I obey, wondering how the hell she did that. She grips my arm, but it doesn't hurt. She checks up and down the walkway to make sure we're alone, then presses her armored hand to the smooth golden wall. An invisible seam opens with a moan, resembling a tear in thin fabric. She yanks me through, and the seam closes behind us until it's just a wall again, which should surprise me more than it does. We're in a small, circular, featureless room with no light source, and yet I can see. The soft light seems to come from the walls themselves.

She says, "We need to make this fast. What is the status of your world?"

I open my mouth, but no words come out, my mind racing to catch up. I was in the Oval Office *seconds* ago, and now everything has a gold tint and an Olivia is holding me hostage.

"The status."

She asked about *my* world. She must know who I am. "The eyeless are free," is all I can say.

She closes her eyes. "I can't help you. Not directly." She holds up the broken length of metal that used to be the Torch. "Repairing this will take too long."

Everything clicks, and I realize who stands before me—the Olivia who visited Noble, who told him the truth and positioned him in Commander Gane's world.

The Original Olivia.

She doesn't wait for me to respond.

"Director Miranda has another Torch. Obtaining it would be nearly suicidal, but there's no other way to save your world."

A moment passes. I shrug and say, "I have nothing better to do." But I don't feel the words.

She doesn't buy my bravery. "Do you know where you are?"

"True Earth."

"Yes. The Torch is designed to return to me if it's broken in the field. But acquiring the second one from the director isn't the hardest part."

She doesn't have to tell me. "Destroying the eyeless."

"Yes."

"Commander Gane told me what to do. He told me how to destroy them in the Verge."

"Good."

"But I'll die."

Olivia nods. "That's true. But you'll save the world."

I clench my hands into fists and tremble. I want to scream. I want to hit her calm, placid face. "There has to be another way."

She shakes her head. "There isn't. Killing all of them at once would require you to be close enough with the Torch. And once they feel threatened, even you won't be able to control them. It has to happen all at once. You must lure them."

"I don't want to do it."

I want my chance to live. From the day I opened my eyes,

it's been *this*. But I'm silly for saying I don't want to, because I know I will.

She knows it too.

I always wondered if there was going to be more to my life, and now I know there isn't. It'll be over soon, and I won't have to fight anymore.

"And when the eyeless are gone, what will True Earth do then?" I say. I need to know this won't be for nothing. I need someone to say I existed and then died for a reason.

"They won't stop, but it will buy us time."

"What if I fail?"

"Then your universe belongs to them. So you won't fail."

Right then I let go of everything.

"I have to get back before I'm missed," Olivia says, "but I need to reopen that scar on your cheek so it seems fresh. We don't have scars in our world."

Before I can protest, she lifts a knife to my face and drags it across the scar from Mrs. North. I feel no pain at first, just pressure. Hot blood rolls down my cheek.

"Good." Then, rapid-fire, she says, "Now go. The Rose Tower is just around the bend—you'll know it when you see it. Put your hand on the wall to get inside. Tell some-one you were attacked. If anyone asks your number, it's M-two-four-zero-seven. Remember that. Act like you belong there, because nobody can prove you don't. Once you have the Torch, you can use it to return home just by thinking about it. Understand?"

"Yes," I say, while still absorbing her words. My stinging cheek actually helps. The pain focuses me.

She puts her hand on the wall and a seam splits open, showing me a world I couldn't have dreamed.

"One more thing," she says. "Take this."

She takes my hand and turns it over, then presses a small black square the size of a stamp into my palm. It adheres to the armor, then dissolves into a liquid my suit somehow absorbs. A second later, I feel it push through the skin of my palm in a way that's somehow pleasant.

"What was that?"

"If you find yourself against uneven odds, make a fist as hard as you can. Now go."

I step through the seam, and it seals shut behind me.

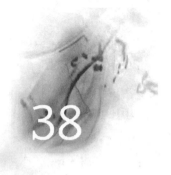

38

The air smells like pine and hot metal, the same scent I experienced when the Torch first started buzzing on the floor of the Oval Office.

I spend twenty seconds taking stock of my surroundings with a tactical eye, committing the area to memory. It's nothing I could've imagined, not in a million years. I'm on a long, winding walkway. At the railing, the ground is just an idea far below. Up here are golden towers, impossibly wide, connected by covered bridges and open walkways. Each tower is rounded and smooth, no hard angles, like polished stalagmites made of gold, rising what feels like miles from the earth.

Everything is gold, the sky included. An unnatural sky, yet rich and deep and beautiful. If there were clouds, they'd be made of honey.

I lean over the railing, searching harder for the ground.

"What are you doing up here?"

I push away from the railing and try to hide how startled I am.

It's Noah. But not my Noah. He wears the same armor as me, black, but pristine. Clearly he hasn't seen combat. His eyes widen as he takes in my battered face and chewed-up armor.

"What the hell happened to you? What's your number?"

"M-two-four-zero-seven," I say automatically.

"Who attacked you?" he says, pulling a sword off his back. The sword hums and the blade is out of focus. It's vibrating too fast to see clearly. I can only imagine what happens when the edge touches flesh. Behind him, one tower is the color of a rose. It's the only non-gold one in sight.

He checks up and down the walkway. "I asked who attacked you. And why did you let them do that to your face?"

His tone isn't familiar, and it's really messing with me, since I know the face so well. Blurry-vibro sword or not, I refuse to let my mission end seconds after it begins. I harden my eyes and straighten up to show he isn't intimidating.

"There were three of them," I say, figuring the peaceful way out is a lie.

"Who were they? Were they Peters?"

At first I think he means that in the possessive, as in, *Did the attackers belong to Peter?*, but then I realize he means *Were they actual Peters?*, as in plural. And right then it becomes clear that my number 2407 might mean I'm one of at least 2407 Mirandas. If I had to bet, I have a good idea which tower they're all in.

I assume he's asking because the Peters have been known to do this. Or maybe the Noahs just don't like the Peters. . . .

"Yes," I say. "They were Peters."

"Of course they were. Do you remember their numbers?"

"No, I—"

Without warning, he shoves me up against the tower wall, and I have to stop myself from putting an elbow through his nose. He pulls a little laser pointer from a pouch on his hip and shines it into my eye. "Keep it open!" he growls when I squint. I force my eyes open and he goes, "Hmm."

"Hmm what?"

He brings his wrist to his lips. "I have M2407 wandering around on the high decks outside the Rose Tower. Claims she was beaten by a trio of Peters. Her armor is damaged. Please advise." He waits a few seconds. I slouch against the wall, feeling embarrassed despite myself. He seems disgusted I let a couple of Peters get the best of me. "She tests positive for a memory swap, yes. Yes." He focuses on me again. "What were you doing out here?"

"I don't remember. They hit me in the head a few times." I tenderly touch above my right ear and fake-wince. He's so unlike my Noah. There's no hint of playful mischief in his eyes, just intensity. It's Noah's face, his body, but everything underneath is different.

He notices me studying him. "What is it?"

"Nothing."

His eyes unfocus when he listens to a voice I can't hear. "Affirmative," he says. Then, to me, "Head to the infirmary, the one on level ninety. They want to take a download from you to see the attackers."

I don't think so. That would end things really fast. "I didn't see them at all. They jumped me and I couldn't see well after they broke my nose." My nose is swollen enough to *look* broken, complete with dried blood.

"Then how did you know they were Peters?"

"I just knew."

He sighs. "Please go. Don't make this difficult for me."

At least I'm going inside the Tower. I start to walk down the path, metal ringing softly under my feet. I feel the Noah's eyes on my spine. Behind the Rose Tower, a sleek helicopter rises above the building and banks away from me.

The walkway peels off from the golden building and becomes a long open bridge to the Rose Tower. My pulse rises the closer I get.

The circumference of the Rose Tower has to be longer than a half mile; this close, it fills my vision, too big to see all at once. The rose-colored metal is dull, not brilliant like the towers surrounding me. I approach the wall and look over my shoulder—the Noah is still watching me from the other end of the bridge.

"Open it!" he calls.

There's nothing to open, so I do what Olivia did. I put my hand on the wall and think *Open* in my mind, in case I'm supposed to, and the wall parts beneath my hand. When I look back, the Noah is gone. I step through into a small room with an elevator door and nothing else. It's as though the room just appeared for me exactly where I needed it.

The door opens into a cylinder-shaped car. I step inside, and a smooth male voice says, "Level."

"Ninety," I reply.

My feet glue to the floor with two metallic thrums, which I appreciate, because one second later the car slips into free fall.

The infirmary is a large room two levels tall. It feels sterile and cold and uncomfortable, unnecessarily big. Beds line the walls, a few of them occupied with people I recognize but don't know. Two Olives, a Miranda, four Rhyses, *six* Peters, one Noah. People like my friends, but probably totally unlike them at the same time. Most of them are in slender arm or leg casts

266

that give off a pale glow, with wires trailing to what look like white plastic server towers. The towers project holographic images above each Rose, displaying vitals that are perfectly visible no matter where I stand.

A completely hairless man in a white lab coat approaches. He's smiling at me warmly.

"What's the matter, dear?"

He holds his arm up, presenting the back of his hand to me. I have no idea what I'm supposed to do with it. When he gets close enough, I lightly touch the back of my hand to his, which he accepts.

"You've had a battle," he says, leaning in and squinting. "Do you know who I am?"

I hesitate, which he probably mistakes for brain damage.

"I'm Dr. Delaney. You're M-two-four-oh-seven?"

"I am."

"Very good. The two thousands are a fine group. Can you tell me what happened?"

"Three Peters jumped me," I say automatically.

He makes a noise of disapproval in his throat. "That rivalry needs to stop." He takes my hand and leads me to an open bed, where I sit down and almost collapse. The bed is so soft it nearly swallows me.

"Now, I'd like to take a memory download from you for the next few days, just to see how things are tracking."

My throat tightens. A download for the next few days sounds okay, but if he sees my memories leading up to this, even *looks* at them, my trip here will be over.

"I'll take a full imprint too, if that's all right." He's pressing buttons on the face of the white server tower next to my bed, but sees my face fall. "Don't worry, I won't look at them. Just a precaution. It's good to have clean backups if damage is present."

"Okay," I say. Because how else can I respond? Even if I want to scream, *NO, YOU CAN'T HAVE MY IDENTITY!* the other Roses in the beds don't seem to notice me, or care. If I had to fight Delaney on the full download, would they all attack?

Delaney shines a light into my eyes. "Now that is a broken nose," he says.

Eyeless are killing people *right now*, I have no idea how I'm going to find the Torch and get home, and Dr. Delaney is treating me with kindness. I need hard and cold and evil right now if I'm going to stay sharp.

"Relax. This won't hurt." He shows me a strip of metal with a thick wire trailing from it. "Have you ever used this before?"

"No." I remind myself he's not here to hurt me, but to help. "What is it?"

"It's better to show you," he says, lifting the strip to my nose and pressing it to the skin. Something clicks in my nose—I

268

guess it really was broken. The dried blood in my sinuses evaporates, and I can breathe again. The bruises and scrapes all over my body dwindle to nothing, leaving me in a warm glow. In a few seconds, I feel like a million bucks. Bone-tired, but without pain.

The strip of metal has turned rust-orange. "There, see? Not bad." I still feel blood and sweat dried on my skin and hair, but that's nothing a shower can't fix. "You'll find new armor in the showers. Toss that one."

"Okay." I slip off the bed, happy to be free. And actually grateful for his help.

"Wait one." He comes over with a small disk the size of a quarter, stamped with the letter M. He turns me around by the shoulders, pulls aside my hair, and sticks the disk against the base of my skull before I realize what it's for. The disk feels cool for a second, then melts to warmth, spreading into my brain. "Return that next week and we'll have a look. You don't have to take your shots while it's on. However, if you feel ill tonight, come back and see me. If you still have memory problems, come back and see me. Got it?"

"Thanks, doctor." So the disk will store my memories. All I have to do is not give it back and our secrets will stay safe.

"My pleasure, dear." He turns away and moves to a different bed. I'm free.

The realization that I have no idea where to go settles on

me like a lead dress. I walk to the elevator, feeling a little dizzy with the task before me. Finding the director is one thing; getting the Torch away from her—and surviving—is another. For all I know, she sleeps with it.

The elevator doors open, and a Rhys stands there. A Rhys with battered armor and a familiar smile. His eyes hold recognition.

I keep staring at him. It can't be. . . .

"Yeah," he says. "It's me. Why has everyone been asking for my number? Like I'd want any of these assholes to call me."

Despite the ongoing apocalypse, I almost burst into laughter. I manage to contain myself and step into the elevator. Dr. Delaney gives me a friendly wave from the bed of an Olivia. The doors shut, and we throw our arms around each other and hug so tight, the wounds Delaney healed begin to tingle.

"A complete dick move, Miranda."

I pull back to look into his face. He's trying to be stern, but I can tell he's happy to see me. Under all that is a heavy dread, mostly around his eyes.

"How did you get here?"

"You know how long it's been since I've done an endurance sprint? A long time."

"Where's Peter?"

"Level," the elevator says.

"Auditorium," Rhys replies.

The elevator ascends at a normal speed this time. I'm still holding his arms, like I'm afraid he'll disappear if I let go.

"Is he safe?" I say.

"I don't know, to both." He bites his lower lip. "We made it to the Verge and jumped through the Black, and . . . I ended up here. There's a portal just outside. The pill you swallowed showed up on this." He lifts the little tracking device and wiggles it.

Rhys doesn't know.

"What is it?" he says. "Thought you'd be happy to see me."

"The Torch is broken. It broke when I killed Nina. The eyeless are free in our world."

He frowns. "I see."

"So we need to find the director, like now. Maybe together we can overpower her and take her Torch."

"We're heading in the right direction," he says, eyes on the rising numbers. "I passed a few Roses talking about the auditorium. Something is going down. The director will be there. But it sounds like a lot of people will be there—you think a smash-and-grab is the right play?"

Before I can answer, the doors open, and I see exactly why we're going to lose this war.

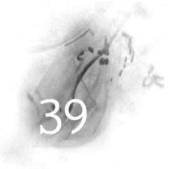

39

The auditorium is larger than anything in my universe. It takes up the entire circumference of the building and looks at least a quarter mile across. Three football fields, closer to four. The rows of seats are hundreds of concentric circles that slope down to the very center, like an ancient Greek theater. In the center a raised dais holds five chairs that resemble thrones more than anything. The whole cylinder-shaped room has to be ten stories tall, bigger than the biggest indoor stadium in my world.

And the auditorium is full.

Nearly every seat is occupied by a Rose in black scaled armor. Some of them are armored in gold scales, or silver. A few are the dusky red of old blood or fresh roses. They must be ranks. The majority are black, though, like us. We wear the armor of the lowest rank, I guess.

There have to be thousands of them, all seated in groups of five. Each team has a version of our Alpha team, all with individual lives and wants and needs and thoughts.

Rhys is silent beside me. When I finally glance at him, he closes his hanging jaw; there's nothing to say.

In unison, everyone stands. A great cheer rises up, deafening, and some of the Roses stomp their armored feet. I feel the vibration in the scales of my suit, in my bones. I scan the crowd for the impetus—a row of five figures walks down one of the aisles to the dais, just close enough for me to tell who they are. They wave at the crowd. All five are dressed in gold scales, with flowing red capes. It's another Alpha team, but they aren't clones—it's the Originals. Olivia is among them, walking in back with the Original Noah. Seeing her gives me a spark of hope that doesn't last; she may claim to be helping me, but it doesn't feel like it from all the way over here. And there's not much more she can do for me.

I find the director leading the way, side by side with the Original Rhys.

Most importantly, the director isn't carrying the Torch. I almost smile, but instead sigh with partial relief. We should go looking for it, but there's no way I can leave, not yet. Rhys was right—something is going down.

273

"She doesn't have it," I tell Rhys.

"I can see that. Let's wait a minute, yeah?"

They climb stairs behind the dais, move to their thrones, and wave to the Roses, who scream and cheer at them, whistling and clapping.

There are a few empty seats in the back row near us. I pull Rhys out of the shadows near the elevator, and we slip into the row. I'm behind an auburn-haired girl—me. Rhys stands behind a version of himself. Farther down the row is another team, but the Peter on the end doesn't spare us a glance. We're without a full team, but at least we're less obvious as part of the group.

"Thank you," the director says, her voice amplified to the entire room. Under the lights, her hair appears blond, not auburn. Not how I remember it from Mrs. North's memory.

Eventually the Roses quiet and begin to sit down. The Originals take their seats together. The distance is too great to make out details, but they look just like us. Young, even though they're impossibly old. Swap their golden armor with black and it would be impossible to tell they're the ruling body of this world. That comforts me. It makes them like us. And if we can die, so can they.

"Thank you," the director says again, stopping all chatter at once. Her voice booms through the auditorium, even though she keeps it soft. There is no echo, just this voice in my ears.

"You know why you are here," she says. An auditorium-wide cheer explodes, and the director has to raise her hands for silence. "You know why you are here, and I thank you, your Mothers and Fathers thank you, for your patience."

The entire curving wall of the auditorium is black.

Suddenly it changes to red.

Rhys slips his fingers around my hand and squeezes. I squeeze back.

Slowly, the red fades into a video of flames, and it's not a wall now, but a screen. A massive wraparound screen, all 360 degrees, that shows cities burning, volcanoes exploding, massive waves hundreds of feet tall crashing onto land. I see versions of New York and Los Angeles. I see cities I don't recognize, gleaming towers taller than anything I've seen yet. Entire cities made of glass, sparkling in the sun. Cities in hollowed-out mountains, entire villages cut into the sides of rocks. The camera pans and swoops, showing a hundred alien places. Worlds that have their own histories and people.

The director says, "For one thousand years, the eyeless have been our protectors. We've guided them through count-less realms. Realms that would do True Earth harm. They have been tireless and efficient. But they will work alone no more."

She waits. Nervous chatter ripples across the auditorium. *One thousand years,* she said. . . . It can't be. The Roses

275

are practically buzzing in their seats. "For as many years, the Roses have guarded this world from those who would destroy it from within. You have been as tireless as the eyeless. As time went on, and our enemies died, your function as protectors of this realm from internal threats became more ceremonial. In short, there are no more enemies to fight. Not here at home."

The Original Peter cuts in, voice booming. "That's what happens when the Roses are given a task. May I remind our lovely director that the Prime rebellion was crushed in *four days*."

That gets laughter from some, hoots and cheering from many. A few nearby Peters slap one another on the chest, charged up from the praise of their Original. The dread in my stomach spreads. Our enemy is ancient and has succeeded against greater worlds. It was easier to know that when the visual proof wasn't on a ten-story-tall screen.

"Yes," the director says, smiling, "thank you for that, Peter. Let us never forget where we came from. Remember we were once like the enemy we now fight. Before us, there was chaos."

Meanwhile, the images continue. They show the eyeless swarming into the cities of different worlds.

Rhys hasn't let go of my hand. He gives it a squeeze and whispers in my ear, "I think we've seen enough. Let's find the Torch."

I look at the dais again. The Originals are weaponless, save for their bodies. I try to imagine them being alive for over a thousand years, and my brain can't process it.

"We should check her office now," he says, squeezing harder.

I feel rooted in place. Seeing all of this—*us*—rejoicing in the destruction of so many lives. Of so many worlds. For what? For what?

Rhys almost stands up, but I clench my fingers around his hand. "Wait." I don't know why I want to see this. I think I have to. Maybe once the dread evaporates, it will leave strength behind.

The director continues. "Not all of you can join us in the fight against this new world. Some will need to remain here to guard the realm, at least for now, until we can rotate teams. So we will ask for volunteers to stay behind. You've all worked very hard for this day, and those who offer will be rewarded. We don't want to have to choose." She looks left and right at the others seated on the dais. I wish I were closer. I wish I could see their faces, the expressions they make. "We haven't settled on a reward yet, but I promise it will be worth it."

"Do you know where the director's office is?" Rhys's voice sounds different. He wants to leave, and badly.

I don't look at him, not wanting to see my fear reflected in his eyes. "No. Wait. Just wait."

The formality seems to have drained from the place. It's

like the pep rally at school, when the teachers would speak to the students and the students were restless in their seats, ready to move. But it's not a joyous occasion. They aren't really pumping themselves up to take on a rival team, though it seems that way. No, the smiles and subtle laughter and back-patting are because they're about to end an entire world.

"I'll go without you. I'll probably get lost," Rhys says.

"No you won't." I wouldn't let him go without me.

"I'm getting up right now."

"Just wait, please." I should've left when Rhys wanted to; something is coming that I don't want to see, I know it. Yet I can't move.

The director isn't finished. Her voice booms, *"Now look upon your enemy!"*

My heart stops as Rhys finally stands up and pulls me out of my seat. I follow him, eyes up on the big screen, as Rhys palm-strikes the elevator button. The doors open and he yanks me inside and pins my arms to the back of the elevator. "Stay put," he says.

Before the doors shut, I catch a glimpse of my world over his shoulder.

The Rose on-screen appears several stories tall. The White House behind him is taller. I know it's him. No doubt in my mind. And it shatters any strength I had left.

Peter is on one knee, covered in blood, surrounded by three eyeless. His sword is blood-soaked and unsteady. They circle him like wolves, claws clicking on concrete.

The elevator doors shut.

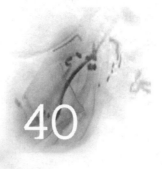

40

I pound on the button to open the door, but we're already rising. So I kick the door, screaming, and Rhys wraps his arms around me in a bear hug until I stop struggling. He squeezes tight, and I have no breath to scream or room to inhale. Then he lets go and I slump against the door, struggling to breathe. The metal is cold against my forehead.

"Level," the elevator says.

"Did I squeeze too hard?" Rhys asks me.

I have no breath to answer. My mind is on fire.

"This is the best way to help him. We get the Torch and go home and stop them. What could we do from the auditorium?" He spins me around and forces me to look at him. "What could we do? Huh?"

"Nothing." He's right. I know he's right, but it does little to calm me. I shove him away. "Why did you leave him?" I spit a little when I say it.

"Level," the elevator says again.

"The director's office," I say.

I don't think it's going to work until the car is suddenly ascending, smooth as silk. My anger doesn't ebb, which isn't a bad thing. It can make me strong if I manage to rein it in.

"Peter is fine," Rhys says. "You saw his face." He knows Peter's resolve, the complete refusal to fail. I would feel sorry for the eyeless he faced, if I were able to.

I see now why Peter's been pulling away from me, why I should be pulling away from him. My feelings for him almost made me charge back into the auditorium. Had it been Rhys, would I have done the same, or would I have kept a cool head and put the mission first? I need to forget about Peter, to trust in his ability.

In the doors, I see a reflection of Noah standing next to Rhys. When I turn, he's gone. Rhys has his eyes closed and doesn't notice my sudden movement.

Go away, I think. Then, *Are you there?*

No response. Great, now I'm seeing things.

We rise for what feels like minutes, fast enough to put strain on my knees. Then suddenly we stop and the doors open to reveal an office—one identical to Commander Gane's. The four walls of the pyramid are made of glass. In Mrs. North's memory, the director had left them tinted, but now I can see the entire golden sky in all directions and, behind her desk, the immense blue sheet of an ocean, as if seen from an airplane.

Rhys doesn't care about the view; he only has eyes for one thing—the Torch resting on the desk. The dull crimson globe hangs over the side.

It's too easy.

Unless the director is so confident that the idea of someone taking it is preposterous.

I step out of the elevator, and Rhys follows.

"Just grab it," he says, looking as weary as I feel. He's right—it's time to get the hell out of here.

I cross to the desk and my fingers hover over the Torch. The staff emits some kind of static I feel in the pads of my fingertips, through my suit.

I hear the elevator doors swish open again.

"Miranda!" Rhys shouts.

I snatch the Torch off the desk and spin, feeling it reach out for nearby eyeless. The bulb flares bright red as five Roses clad in golden armor step out of the elevator. They pull their swords off their backs in unison. Miranda, Noah, Peter, Rhys, Olive, from left to right. They aren't the Originals, just some kind of elite team, I'm guessing.

The Peter steps forward. "Against royal decree six-one-five, you have entered a Mother's or Father's office without express permission. Relinquish the Torch and kneel before us or face the justice of True Earth." He recites it like he's bored. Business as usual.

Rhys looks back at me with raised eyebrows that ask, *Do we give it a shot?*

But we don't get that far. My hand hasn't yet closed around Beacon's grip when a strange static crawls over my skin. The static turns solid in the next second, clamping down on me like a vise. I've felt this sensation before. The Peter has his hands straight out, fingers curled like he's holding two invisible eggs. Slowly, he forces us to kneel.

"We're special," the Miranda says with a smile.

The five encircle us, and then the Noah and Olivia yank my arms back and bind my wrists roughly. The cuffs shrink until my fingers tingle, feeling fat with trapped blood. When the Peter turns for the elevator, I see a bulge between his shoulder blades, under his golden scales. The same power pack Gane used, which has implications I'm not prepared or willing to dissect at the moment.

No one speaks on the ride back down. No one so much as coughs. I spend the time thinking about how we lost.

Noah's voice startles me. "Since when do you quit?"

I don't know what to say.

"You're definitely not the Miranda I knew then."

That stings. My cheeks grow hot. How dare he bring that up when it's *his* fault the girl before me died in that alley.

"Think of a plan," Noah says. "Don't give up. If you're not worried about me up here, worry about Peter. Not to mention the entire world."

Come and go as you please, by all means.

"I'm trying not to distract you. But I never left. I never would. You need to fight. If not you, then who? Who, Miranda?"

I feel him recede into some dark corner again. His absence leaves a void in me, like before.

After a minute, the doors open. The cells are clear plastic cubes with no visible doors and no bars or locks. On the left, two of the walls slide open. Then Noah and Olivia shove me into the first one and Rhys into the second. The doors suck shut behind us; the bindings pop off our wrists and clatter to the floor. I bring my hands around and rub my wrists until the tingling in my fingertips becomes pain. When I turn, the five in gold are gone.

One person occupies the farthest cube in the row, but he's sleeping. I think it's a Noah. Other than him, we're completely alone. Just stark white walls and clear plastic with no obvious seams.

In the next cube over, Rhys rubs his wrists and shakes his head slowly. A tendon bulges in his jaw. The next second, he's at the front of his cube, pounding his fists against the plastic and screaming at the top of his lungs. It's the sound of primal rage, and I remember we're not so helpless. Set us free and we're as deadly as any of the Roses from the auditorium. Maybe more so. We have something to fight for, after all.

Rhys punches the wall between us. The plastic makes a snapping thud, and he steps back, shaking his hand out.

"Feel better?" I say.

He only has to raise his voice a little to be heard. "Not really. But the pain is kind of nice. You should try it." He throws his hands down, disgust all over his face.

"Yeah." Seeing his helplessness mixed with rage makes it easier for me, as terrible as that sounds. Misery loves company, I guess.

"Does Noah have any ideas?" Rhys says. "He's still in there, right?"

"Let me ask him."

"No," Noah says.

"No," I say.

Rhys looks befuddled, and then he laughs. "Did he—did he even think about it?" he says between laughs.

I'd laugh if I had the energy. Seeing Rhys laugh makes it impossible not to smile, though.

"Tell him I say hi. Tell him he owes me five bucks from that bet last week. I'll take it from his sock drawer."

"Hi, Rhys. Touch my money and I'll haunt you."

For some reason, that makes my chest seize.

You're not a ghost.

"Not yet."

"He says..." I trail off as pressure builds against the back of my eyeballs. I will not cry.

I will not cry.

The main door opens behind me, and a pair of visitors comes through. Two Originals, shining golden scales and red cloaks to their heels.

The director and the Original Rhys.

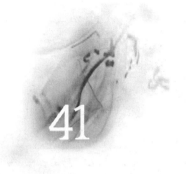

41

Rhys's Original looks exactly like Rhys, no older or younger. His blond hair is slicked back and longer, curling away from his neck, not the sideways part Rhys prefers. I can see hundreds of my tiny reflections in the golden scales of his armor. His eyes have the same ancient quality as the director's. It's hard not to feel awe in the presence of beings who have lived for over a thousand years. I don't want to be in awe; I want to look down on them. Or I want to feel equal. I know now how they got the auditorium into such a fervor. They seem utterly sure, utterly competent, all in the way they carry themselves. It's an energy that fills the room. They aren't quite smiling, but they look happy. Content. And they should be, since they're among the five most powerful people in all the universes.

They appraise us in silence for thirty seconds. To our credit, we don't say a word, just return the stare. The back of my neck begins to itch. The director's hair really is golden, not auburn. I guess the tacky cloak isn't enough to set her apart from her clones.

"What do we do with them?" the Original Rhys finally asks.

Let us free. Give us a chance to fight. I ignore the actual possibilities. But it strikes me that maybe, just maybe, they underestimate us. And maybe I can use that.

The director watches me with a hint of disappointment on her otherwise blank face. "What were you doing in my office?"

They don't know who we are. I could still be Miranda 2407 to them.

Rhys opens his mouth and utters a syllable, but I interrupt him. "I wanted to see the Torch. I'm sorry."

My palm itches where the black square dissolved through my armor. I think about making a fist as hard as I can, but now might be the wrong time.

The director rolls her eyes. "Please. I know who you are."

So I was wrong, but if the director is really so wise, if she's moved beyond things like hate, maybe I can reason with her. And no matter what, I know she underestimates my resolve.

I can't stop myself from the moment of weakness that comes

next, because I have to try, no matter how unlikely it is. I was never much for begging, but now I press my hands against the plastic and feel my face contort. "Please," I say. "Please stop. We can make some agreement. You can close the way to our world. You'll never hear from us again."

Original Rhys says, "The way can never be fully closed. All worlds aggressive and unenlightened are purged before they can grow beyond our control. Your world is aggressive and unenlightened."

I pound my fists on the glass, hard and sharp. They don't flinch. "And you can't figure out a better way to control us? *Monsters?* You send animals into our world to *eat us*. You..." I want to go on, but there is no emotional change in their faces. I might as well be screaming at robots. I guess after doing this for a thousand years, it's hard to care at all. The end for us is a normal day for them.

"The eyeless ensure the world is intact for future genera-tions. For repopulation on our terms, with careful control," Original Rhys says. I catch a peek of Rhys from the corner of my eye. He stares at his progenitor with pure hatred.

"We pose no threat to you. My world doesn't even know about the Black." My voice is smaller than I'd like. The urge to reason with them drains out of me like blood through a thousand cuts. Words won't change this. Nothing will change until I'm free with a sword in my hand.

"That's the point," the director says softly. "One day it will."

"We're late," Original Rhys says. Then he smirks at me. "Our monsters have to eat."

"Stop," she tells him, almost playfully. To me she says, "We will speak again upon our return. In the meantime, Dr. Delaney will cull your memories to learn who else stands with you."

And just like that, they're gone. The door hisses shut behind them.

Things get worse after that. Rhys withdraws to a corner of his cube and rubs his fingers against his temples. I know how he feels—like a trapped animal. I pace the small area of my cube at first, trying to think, shoving emotion aside. *A clear mind is an efficient mind*, our Dr. Tycast used to say. Actually, I may have made that up, but it sounds like something he would say.

After a while, Noah appears in the corner and watches me pace. I don't look at him. His dark eyes will be another reminder of the people I've failed.

I visualize the army of Roses crossing over right now, storming into a confused and terrified world already under attack. They are the insult being added to the injury. This different enemy will emerge from nowhere and march in our streets, aiding the monsters in the extermination. People won't just die in agony. They'll die as afraid as they've ever been in their lives.

* * *

"Got anything?" Rhys says after an hour.

An *hour* has passed.

How many dead?

"Got anything?" he says again.

Is this my fault? Is this on me?

"No."

He doesn't ask me a third time.

Dr. Delaney comes in during the second hour. He looks at me like I've betrayed him. I almost feel bad about it, since he helped me, but I never quite get there. He still fights for this side, so he's an enemy.

The five golden Roses who first captured us come back and open the door to my cell; the sudden freedom strikes something in me I can't control. A last-ditch effort, I guess. I charge them as the Peter raises a rifle and shoots me with a dart. It pierces my abdomen, and blood wells behind the armor. The drugs work fast. Heat moves through my veins, branching out like tree limbs. It reaches my brain, and my eyes swim. It doesn't quite put me to sleep, but I'm weak enough for them to drag me back to the infirmary.

I fade in and out, catching glimpses of the hallway they drag me down. The way is paved in gold. Must be a pretty common element here. Or they have a gold paint surplus. Once I see the bed with straps, I try to kick and punch and bite, but by then the poison has made it through my entire system. The best I can manage is a moan. Rhys is slumped between two Roses on the other side of the room. *Don't strap us down,* I want to say. *Leave us alone. We're just like you.*

They get me on the bed and strap my ankles and wrists to the frame.

"Leave her armor on?" someone says.

"I only need her from the neck up. It's fine."

Delaney's face comes into view, blocking the light from the ceiling. "Hello, Miranda. I'm going to take your memories from you now. If you could relax your mind, that would be ideal. I don't want this to hurt."

Olivia's words echo in my mind. *If you find yourself against uneven odds . . .*

I'd say this is pretty uneven.

Make a fist, she said, *as hard as you can.*

I make a fist as hard as I can.

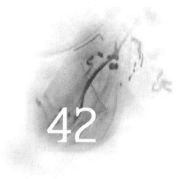

42

The result is instantaneous. The heat that courses up my arm is different from the poison. This is a lightning strike, hot and electric. At first I wonder why I didn't do this sooner. My heart pounds so hard I feel it thumping against the inside of my ribs. Each breath gives me strength, until I feel like I'm bursting out of my suit. My vision flickers red with every heartbeat.

I lift my arms and the straps around my wrists break like strings. I sit up and pull the ones off my ankles. Delaney spins around and drops his tray of instruments. The five golden Roses pull the swords off their backs and hold them high. The Peter is just lifting his arm, but he's slow, so slow.

I pick up the bed and throw it at them.

It knocks three of them over. They skid all the way across the floor, toppling more beds. The remaining two come at me swinging, but their strikes are in slow motion. The one over-hand chop from the Noah is laughable. I step around him before his chop is finished, then punch him at the base of his skull. The crunch travels up my forearm. The Miranda stabs at my belly, but I bend out of the way and backhand her so hard it snaps her neck. She collapses, and I catch her sword before it hits the ground.

The Peter and the Olive are unconscious. But the Rhys shoves the twisted bed off himself and stands up, sword raised.

"Drop it," I tell him. He doesn't. I sidestep his thrust and run past his right, dragging my blade across his throat.

When it's over, I stand in the middle of the infirmary, heaving, searching for a new target. The other clones occupying beds watch me with wide eyes, waiting to see what I'll do next, but they aren't my concern. Delaney is hiding behind one of the overturned beds. My strength fades, and I'm left sick on wobbly feet.

Rhys is strapped to a bed, like I was. His stares at me, mouth hanging open.

I don't feel a thing besides my amped blood. The people in my world are dying in much worse ways right now.

"Cut me free," Rhys says. His voice is hoarse.

I tug at his straps, but my artificial strength is gone. I have to use the bloody sword to cut him out. He slips off the bed and checks pulses, then appropriates weapons.

"You'll have to tell me how you did that," he says.

Suddenly I can barely stand. The strength leaving me seems to take some of my natural strength too. I lean against the bed, and Rhys puts his hand on my back.

"Thank you for saving me," he says. "Are you okay?"

No, I'm not. I look at the mess I've made and begin to feel. I can't know if they were evil or if they were raised to do this one job, like we were, until we knew better. But if they had good in them, they would have known better. Their upbringing and superiority is no excuse for planet-wide extermination. Not even close.

"Don't think about it," Rhys says. "We'll think later, yeah?" He tucks a sweaty strand of hair behind my ear, then cups my face until I look into his eyes. They burn bright now.

"We have a world to save," he says.

I summon what strength I have left and renew it with hope. We are free, and nothing is going to stop us.

We ride back to the auditorium. The Roses are funneling out through an exit at the far end. The Originals are gone. Rhys and I hover near the back of the Roses lining up to leave. No one really looks at us. The teams of five seem to stick to themselves, chatting in excited tones about what lies ahead. I know what lies ahead; I've seen it.

You there? My strength ebbs like a tide, leaving my balance unsteady. My vision flickers black every few minutes, like I lose consciousness for a thousandth of a second. I wonder if using that disk thing Olivia gave me has long-term side effects. I wonder if I'll live long enough to experience them.

"I'm here," Noah says.

Are you still with me? Till the end?

"I am, but it's hard. You aren't doing it on purpose, but your mind doesn't like me in here. It feels like ... trying not to drown with someone tugging your legs from underwater."

He must feel the horror that rises up in me. "Not your fault, I said. Don't make this about you."

His tone almost makes me smile. He could always joke in the worst situations.

"It was Nina too," he says. "Fighting her took something out of me. I'm in pieces here."

I want to make him whole again. He saved my identity. My *life.* Without him inside my head, I would be Nina right now.

The mass of Roses moves forward another few feet; they're narrowing into a tunnel up ahead. We hang back far enough that no one talks to us.

If I get the Torch —

"You said that. I'm ready. I'm ready and I'm here with you."

It means I'll die.

"I'm here with you."

But he's not. The next second I feel him evaporate. Each time it happens, I wonder if he'll come back. I should find some way to transfer him into a new body. As soon as he came back, he'd be happy. He'd be happy to be alive, to breathe air and see things with his own eyes.

If only I had more time.

I hear a footstep behind me and whirl, hand reaching for my sword. Olivia stands a few feet away, half hidden in the shadows, with a Black portal wide behind her. The red cloak is the only thing that keeps me from cutting her down.

"You're going the wrong way," she says.

I lower Beacon. "What are you doing here?"

She sighs. "Assembling the only hope your world has. I have no time."

"What?" Rhys says helpfully.

"Either come or stay here. I have to get back before my absence is noted."

She steps backward through the portal and disappears, as silent as stepping behind a curtain.

"I don't—" Rhys begins.

His voice cuts off as I step through the Black, pulling him along.

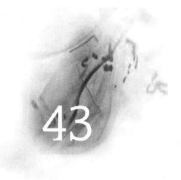

43

The next second, I stand in the school gymnasium. *Our* school gymnasium, outside Cleveland. The last time I was here, it was dark and full of students, and I danced with Peter and Noah. And the DJ made an announcement, and the girl we knew as Sequel became Nina. Now it's bright and empty, save for Peter and Noble and Sophia, who are gathered at half court. Seeing them alive brings me joy I've never felt before, a temporary salve for my wounds, the deeper ones that aren't flesh.

Peter sits with his legs tucked under him, holding his arm in his lap. His armor is gone from the elbow down, ripped away, and his forearm is wrapped in bloody bandages. I go straight to him and kneel and press my lips to his. He has the strength to reach up and touch my hair lightly.

"Missed you," he says against my lips.

"I'm leaving," Olivia says. I turn around and she looks directly at me. "The director will meet with your creators at the top of Key Tower just before dawn to discuss plans for the new government. She will have the Torch. It will be the last chance you have to take it before the eyeless make it this far west. Send them back and destroy them. The Originals won't dare use the Roses without the eyeless. It will buy you time."

"I was close to the Originals," I say. "Why can't you kill them yourself? What are you *waiting* for?"

There's too much anger in my voice; this immortal girl risked herself to reunite us, after all. Her eyes soften and I see the forgiveness before I can apologize.

"It's never that simple. The Originals back up their identities every second, in real time. Kill them, and they will just be born again. Right now there are a dozen versions of themselves in hibernation, just in case they're needed. And so for now, you must do what you can."

Silence falls as we absorb that. More good news.

"I'm sorry," Olivia says. "Be at the top of the tower before dawn. It's all I can do for you." She takes a step backward and disappears through the portal, which winks out of existence the second she does.

Noble has his arm around Sophia, who has red claw marks on her cheek and neck. She looks at me with fire in her eyes. "Dawn is a few hours away. I suggest we plan, before all is truly lost." She's wearing her handmade leather armor, a red sleeveless vest and pants, which only reminds me how different this world must seem to her. We're the aliens now, with paved roads and clean water.

"Plan," Rhys mutters. "What plan? The top of Key Tower is a melted mess. I doubt the creators and the *director* will just hand over the Torch."

"We have to try," Peter says, gritting his teeth when Rhys bumps his injured arm.

Rhys cocks his head to the side and squints. "Isn't that your sword arm?"

"Enough," Noble booms. "I will arrange transportation. I suggest you rest. Everything depends on what happens next."

Rhys and Sophia talk while Noble departs. It'd be interesting to watch them, to see if they like each other, but I have different priorities. I guide Peter down the hallway toward the locker room, where the athletic trainers will have stuff to clean his wounds. I can smell the blood and sweat on him. He grimaces with each step.

"Stop hiding your limp," I say.

He stops.

"They cornered me," he says.

"I saw."

"What?"

"Long story."

We hobble down the steps, side by side. Even though I'm helping him, just feeling him against me gives me strength. He's alive. Blood still pumps through his veins.

He tells me the story while I unwrap his bandage, exposing the deep slash underneath. It curves from his elbow halfway to his wrist, the muscle visible within, red and shiny and striated. He sits down on a bench and rests his head against the lockers, head tilted toward the ceiling. When he blinks, tears leak from the corners of his eyes. I kneel in front of him.

"I rescued this family who'd been in a car crash. The eyeless were clawing at the windows, trying to get in. They had broken the windshield and were pulling it out in one piece. But getting close enough meant . . ." He does a sword swinging motion with his good arm.

"This needs stitches," I say. My stomach turns, not because I'm grossed out, but because the wound looks *bad*. Stitches might not be enough. There isn't enough skin left to cover the muscle. I try not to look afraid, so he's not.

"It can wait," he says. "Just bind it tight."

He groans through clenched teeth when I splash the alcohol into the gash, enough to kill whatever disease the eyeless might carry under their claws. The wound continues under his suit, where the ragged armor ends, so I make him shrug his upper half out. I peel the armor down to his waist.

"See?" he says. "No more."

He's right; I can't find any wounds. Just bruises—some purple, some yellowish. Like a painting of twilight. My fingers trace over them gently, and his skin twitches under them. I poke and prod, looking for some little cut that could fester later on.

"Sorry," I say.

He grins. "The pain isn't that bad."

I let my eyes fall back to his arm and continue dressing the wound. It bleeds right through, an ink blot spreading before my eyes. I have experienced more fear in the last few days than I thought possible, but this is different. This is frustration worse than dread. His arm is damaged and I can't fix it, and it's going to kill him.

But I hide all that for his sake. I can be strong for him.

"Tell you what," I say. "Why don't you clean yourself up, and I'll try to find something better. Maybe a needle and thread."

He looks at me for a few seconds too long. "Okay." Then he doesn't move.

"What is it?"

"Is Noah . . . ?"

I turn inward, but he's nowhere in sight. "No. He's not here. He helped me, though. Nina tried to turn me, and it almost worked."

Peter's eyes widen.

"It's okay. Noah was there. When Nina woke herself inside me, we just . . . beat her back. Together."

Peter is nodding, though he seems sad. "I'm glad. I'm glad you're okay."

"Me too."

Something shifts between us. I don't know what.

He licks his lips, then stands up. Slowly, he limps past the lockers into the communal shower area, leaving behind three drops of blood on the tile. I push myself to my feet and look through the supplies for a needle and thread, but I already knew there wouldn't be any. I hear him turn on the shower. It runs unbroken for ten seconds, until he gets under the stream.

"There are stalls," he calls to me, "if you want to stop smelling."

I smile. The shower room is already steamy. Peter shampoos himself with one hand and keeps his bad arm above the showerhead. I turn my water on and spin it all the way to lava-hot, then peel my suit off. My left palm is burned deeply, and I only feel the pain now that it's free of my suit. A black square is burned into the skin. Olivia's gift almost killed me, but it brought me here. The mark is a small price to pay.

I wash myself quickly, working days of filth out of my hair and skin. I'm not going to say anything to Peter. If he needs distance, I will give that to him. But I don't know what that'll mean when this is over, if we win and I survive.

Peter finishes first and leaves his stall with his armor slung over his shoulder. He's about to walk past my stall door, but he stops.

"What's up?" My voice shakes, and my heart pounds. I curl my fingers over the top of the door.

"Forgive me," he says. Water drips off the end of his chin.

"For what?"

"I should put you first. But I haven't. I love you."

I never said it back the first time. Now I say, "I love you too."

"And you forgive me?"

"There's nothing to forgive. You needed to keep us alive, and I couldn't be trusted."

He shakes his head. "That doesn't excuse how I treated you. I was cold. Just say you forgive me."

I reach over the door and gently pull his lips to mine. He kisses me back, once, softly, but it's different. Noah sharing my mind changes everything. Until we figure out what to do with him, things won't be normal. I start thinking about the rest of our lives, all of us, when the fighting is done. Peter's kiss is different, but there's hope in it. If we survive this, we'll get past it. We can get past anything.

"I want to open the door," Peter says with a shadow of a smile.

"I do too." And I really do.

"But we shouldn't."

I nod and bite my lip. "Peter, when this is over and we have our lives back, we can talk. We can talk about exactly what we want. We just have to win first."

The words taste like a lie, even as I try to believe them myself. If everything happens the way it should, I'll be dead soon. And if it doesn't, I'll be dead soon.

It might be the first time I acknowledge it, truly.

To win, I am going to die.

And I'm afraid.

Peter kisses me one more time, and it's the way it was before, suddenly and magically, and I want to cry and throw open the door and let him hold me, and tell him what I'm planning, and make him say he'll go with me, that we can die together.

But I don't.

"We'll talk," I say. "I love you."

He smiles. "That sounds good."

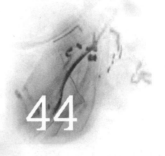

44

The city is empty.

A siren keens in the distance, like the one in D.C. It rises and falls. Word has spread about the invasion, and people have either fled or gone home to cower behind locked doors.

The five of us ride through the empty streets in a school bus, going over a plan that depends on the element of surprise and an escape that depends on insanity.

As we left the school, Peter and Rhys joked about something that happened last week, when things were as normal as they were ever going to get. I sat with Noble near the front. I made him agree to do something for me, something hard. He promised. With the plan set, I was able to relax for the final twenty minutes. I felt my heart beat in my chest and wondered how many beats I had left. If I failed, I would die. If I succeeded, I would die. If today was the day for me to die, it was going to be on my terms.

I waited for Noah to make an appearance, but I couldn't feel him anywhere. When I was talking to Peter, I feared he would return, but he never did. It's sickening to think, but I'm glad he's gone so he doesn't have to see what happens next. So he doesn't have to die twice.

Noble parks a block from Key Tower, hiding the bus behind a hotel. The cap is still a ruined mess, but if Olivia says the meeting will take place there, I believe her. We pile out of the bus, full of nervous energy. To the east, the sky is purple-black. Sunrise isn't far away. Hunger and thirst gnaw at my stomach, but I have a little strength left. I can go a little longer. Maybe I can see the sunrise once more.

We climb to the top, slow and steady, pausing to regain our strength every fifteen floors or so. It gives me time to dwell. I don't think so much about what I'm leaving behind, but what I'm going to miss. Exploring my love with Peter. Growing older. Maybe having a family, or a job.

Of course, all of that hinges on our world being the way it was before, and I don't think it can ever be the same.

Time is a blur until we reach the top floor. The ceiling is warped and sagging in places, a result of the H9 we used to melt the place down. The last time we stood here, Noah and Olive were alive.

I can hear voices above us, distorted through a jagged hole in the ceiling.

In the dim light of the stairwell, Rhys gives me a nod. Noble does too. Sophia smiles, and Peter gives my hand a squeeze.

I grab a jutting piece of metal within the hole and haul myself up.

The roof is a mess of lumpy fused steel, as though the top floors had melted halfway to liquid, then cooled before they could lose shape completely. Which is exactly what happened. The sky is unobstructed in all directions, but it isn't boiling black like Commander Gane's world. It isn't golden, either, like True Earth. It's purple and full of stars. My true sky.

Three people stand in the center, where the floor is most even. Two of our creators wear fresh versions of our black armor—Peter and Olive. They're the same age as Noble, as old as our parents would be if we had any. Mrs. North and the elder Noah are absent. The last person is the director. She holds the Torch in her right hand. The ball glows bright red, reflecting off the shiny scales of her suit. The light turns her golden scales into rubies.

For the first time in a long time, I am without fear.

Though I hide in the shadows, the director somehow knows I'm here. She turns around, along with the creators, and her eyes settle on my hiding place.

"I've never met a daughter so resilient." She doesn't try to hide the awe on her face.

I step out of the dark and pull Beacon from my back.

"She and her friends have caused us some trouble recently," the elder Olive says. We searched for the creators for so long, and now here they are, and it doesn't even matter. They are the least of our worries—pawns, like us.

The director laughs. "I've spent eons controlling thousands of Roses, and you three couldn't control a few teams of five."

I release a wave of fear on the off chance it will affect the creators. They look mildly discomforted, but it doesn't send them running.

"That's the spirit," the director says.

Then her eyes widen at something over my shoulder. I turn around and see my team standing behind me.

"Hello, Rhys," the elder Peter says. "Long time."

"Hello," both Rhyses reply.

The elder Olive sneers. "Where have you been, Noble?"

"Here and there," he replies. "Where's Noah?"

"Gone," is all the elder Peter says.

The director thumps the Torch on the roof. "Why did you come?" She seems to be asking all of us.

"I doubt that's a real question," Peter says next to me.

The elder Peter wears a bulky glove like the Original Olivia. Lightning quick, he draws a circle in the air behind him, and the Black emerges, hovering vertically in the air.

"Don't you dare flee," the director says to him.

Noble pulls a revolver and shoots the elder Peter just as he's stepping backward into the Black. As he falls into the portal, we charge. Gunshots ring out and get swallowed by the sky, but I only have eyes for the director.

She swings the Torch at me like a baseball bat, and I can't avoid the hit to my ribs, because she's faster. It knocks the wind out of me, but I get my hands on the Torch as I fall away. As soon as my fingers touch the staff, the eyeless scream in my mind, annoyed by the presence of another. Every instinct screams, *Let go!* while every thought screams, *Hold on!*

The director pivots, trying to swing me off the Torch like I'm some dog that won't give up its toy, but I hold on. My feet drag over the rough, uneven floor, toes scrabbling for traction. She stops at the end of her swing, eyes flaring angrily, and brings her leg up to kick me off. That's when I pull the Torch to me in one violent motion, snapping my head forward at the same time. The head-butt glances off her chin, but it's enough to loosen her grip on the Torch. I rip it from her grasp and feel the eyeless presence double in my head, a sudden weight around my ears and on top of my skull. Countless minds turn their eyes toward me, the intruder. I feel their hunger. The emptiness is so black and immense that I understand them. I know why they have to feed on world after world. It's the only thing that eases their pain.

My feet are moving away from the director the second I'm free.

Stop, I tell the eyeless. *STOP,* I think. Then I scream, "I GOT IT!" at the top of my lungs. The elder Olivia is dead on the floor. The portal is still black and steady against the purple sky, but the elder Peter is gone.

I sprint for the edge of the roof. The director catches me two feet away and screams in victory. Her fingers dig into my shoulders, pulling me back, but I turn around and lift her up in a bear hug and carry her the final foot. One step is on solid ground, and the next is air.

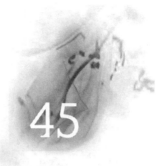

45

We fall over the side as I bash the Torch's shaft into the director's mouth. Her lips split and blood spatters her cheeks. I shake the Torch from her hands and piston off her chest with both feet, then tuck into a backflip in midair.

We fall toward the empty city below. The roaring wind is almost peaceful until the director's rage-soaked scream rattles my head. She's ten feet away, drifting farther as we plunge, but even now her fingers are grasping for me. Then she claps her hands together, never taking her eyes off me. A portal opens in the air below her, and she falls through and disappears.

I fall alone, halfway down the building now, a few seconds from a death too early, until I pull the cord on my parachute.

It snaps open so hard the Torch almost slips from my grip. The straps around my shoulders and waist pinch as I slow down, and the rushing wind becomes a gentle breeze, quiet enough to hear my pulse. Rhys laughs above me, drifting down on his own chute.

Now that I alone hold the Torch, the eyeless stop trying to make my brain explode. I reach out to them. In snapshots, I see the terrible things they do. A herd of them run down the sidewalk in a quiet, upper-class development, splitting off and running across lawns and throwing themselves through bay windows. A trio of eyeless climb the stairs of an office building, preying on the late workers floor by floor. A fire truck tips over as twenty eyeless barrel into it from the side and swarm over it like ants. They leave blood flowing from the broken windows.

There aren't words to describe the horror, but my outrage lends me the power I need to control them. In my mind, I gather up the monsters and show them where to go. I scream it at them. I inject all my will into the order. They know the Verge. I tell them to fill it up and wait. I promise more flesh, more screams.

And they listen. They bend to my will. They stop what they're doing and slink away.

I touch down next to Key Tower, clutching the metal rod to my chest. The globe at the end of the Torch is too bright to look at, a small sun that paints the whole street red.

Now that I have it, it's real. I never thought I'd get this far, not really. I have the eyeless, and I have to follow through. The world and so many others depend on it. *This isn't your last morning,* I tell myself. I have to believe I'm not marching to my death. Peter will see me again, and he'll kiss me again. I will find a way out.

The others land around me, and our chutes billow in the light breeze. The mood is sour, but it should be victorious. We won the best way we could. And we will continue to fight until those who died today are avenged.

Sophia grins. It might be the first time I've really seen her smile.

"We did it," Peter says, hands on his knees, smiling too. "You got it, Miranda."

Noble brings the bus around and opens the door. We pile in, and Noble floors it before we sit down.

I make sure to sit closer to the rear than the others.

"We draw straws," Rhys says after the first block. "Miranda isn't going back."

Poor Rhys. He has no idea.

"No," Peter says, "she isn't."

Poor Peter. He has no idea.

Don't cry; don't let them see the truth.

"I'll draw," Sophia says with steel in her voice.

I wish I could tell them what's about to happen. I wish I could say good-bye the right way.

"No one is drawing," I say. Noble's eyes find mine in the mirror. He gives a slight nod—he'll follow through. I love him for it.

Peter's face is as angry as I've ever seen it, nose and brow crinkled. "Yes, we are."

I shake my head. "I will kill anyone who tries to take this from me. I promise you."

Peter rises out of his seat like an animal and stalks toward me. He grabs the Torch, and his eyes widen as the eyeless fill his mind. I lean forward and kiss him quickly on the lips, then shove him with all the strength I have left. He stumbles down the aisle and lands hard on his back.

"What are you doing?" Rhys says.

What the hell. I kiss him on the cheek too, then nod at Sophia. I would've liked to know her. Noble slams on the brakes and the bus skitters to a stop, tires chuffing on the pavement, old brakes squealing. I run to the back, fling open the emergency exit, and jump down into the cool morning air. Peter's cry of "Miranda!" cuts off when I slam the door.

Noble hits the gas again and leaves me in a cloud of diesel exhaust. I stand in the empty street with the Torch and watch the bus get smaller and smaller until it's out of sight.

❉　❉　❉

I allow myself to cry in the empty street. *This is what you wanted,* I tell myself. *You never liked this life anyway.* But that's not completely true. I loved my friends. I loved Peter and Rhys and Noah and Olive. I hated our purpose, that's all. I hated the reason we existed in the first place.

You wanted a different life.

But I didn't want my life to be over.

Olivia told me the Torch would be able to take me home, but can it take me back to the Verge? What was it she said? It can return me with thought alone. Thought—I can try that.

I close my eyes and focus on the hot metal through my gloves. I feel the eyeless moving toward their doom under my command. I focus hard on the cavern where I first saw the Black, imagining it, but when I open my eyes, I'm still here in the empty street.

"What do I do?" I whisper.

I try again, imaging the inside of Gane's Verge. With that thought in my mind, I hear a footstep behind me and whirl on the balls of my feet.

The director stands before me, sword raised and gleaming in the early dawn, a Black portal behind her. I was foolish to think she'd let me go that easily. Now there's no thought, only movement.

I duck under her slash, dropping straight to my knees. Strands of severed hair flutter down around my shoulders.

She screams another wordless scream of frustration, continuing her spin and coming around for a lower strike I won't be able to dodge. I'm on my knees before her, at her mercy. But it can't end this way. We came too far, at a cost too high.

So I bend forward, until my shoulder touches the ground and I'm rolling past her, out of the way of her second strike, popping to my feet behind her and falling through the very portal she came through.

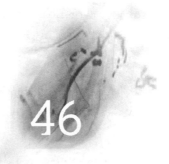

46

At the bottom of the Verge, I think about what I'm going to miss.

Everything. Every moment that was supposed to come.

I sit near the border of the Black with my knees drawn up, clutching the Torch as eyeless surge out of the hole and climb the rough rock walls with their claws. Flakes of rock drift down and ping the metal walkway around me. Some of them bounce off my head like hail. When I went through the portal, I had this place fixed in my mind. And it worked. Just a few minutes ago I was on a bus with the only people I love in this world, and now I'm here, at the end.

I want more time. I keep expecting the director to find me

here, but she doesn't show. Either she doesn't know where I am, or she's afraid to come, knowing I'm in control of her monsters.

The eyeless crowd the levels high above me, not making much noise besides the click and scratch of their claws. Some of them are curious about me. They know I'm the Torchbearer. *What is she doing all the way down there?* they think. *Why did she bring us here? What does she want us to eat? When will there be meat for us?*

A few of the bored ones wrestle, rolling around on the floor, jaws snapping at soft stomachs.

"You're not alone, Miranda."

I look up. Noah stands next to me on the walkway, as real as he's ever been. I'm not alone. But my death means a second one for him. I did this to him, and it's too late to free him from my mind.

"I'm sorry I put you in my mind. To make you live like this."

He just shakes his head, and I know I don't have to be sorry.

"I'm glad," he says softly.

The eyeless continue to well from the Black, so many of them that they crawl on one another, a living, moving ladder. They bubble out like boiling water, and there's no space left. I have to climb before they bury me.

"I wanted to have a job," I say. "I wanted to have a family."

Noah doesn't say anything, for which I'm grateful.

"But I guess now so many others will be able to, if I do this."

He still doesn't say anything.

"Funny how that doesn't make me feel better."

I stand up and stretch my arms above my head.

"You have to climb now," he says.

With one hand on the Torch, I climb up the ladder to where the main floor used to be. When I reach the top, my arm burns. The eyeless skitter away from me, wondering what I'm doing. If they only knew.

I speak the words Gane told me—"Give me a path!"—and a narrow bridge extends from the pillar in the middle. I climb from the ladder onto the walkway, then swing my legs up while keeping a careful grip on the Torch. A few of the eyeless follow me onto the walkway, but I push them back with my mind.

They don't listen. One opens its fanged mouth and hisses at me, saliva dripping from its thin lips. I feel its thoughts. The thoughts spread to the other eyeless roaming the walls and the levels higher above.

They know what I mean to do.

The same eyeless charges me and I raise Beacon and impale it to the hilt. I swing the corpse off and it tumbles toward the Black far below. I step backward into the elevator, and the door shuts as a scream rises up; I feel every eyeless in the Verge turn its attention toward me. Suddenly the Torch is useless. They won't listen. They must be able to override the commands under certain circumstances. Like when the user means to destroy them. Or maybe the director found a way to shut it down remotely. I guess the reason doesn't really matter.

"Bummer," Noah says.

The elevator opens into Commander Gane's office. I step onto the carpet and speak the second set of words. "Give me the light to seal the way."

A safe pops open in the floor. I pull the hatch back and pull out the bomb. It's not such a big thing—it's roughly the size and shape of a bowling ball, with a cord running from it to a small clear pad. The pad has a red button, a green button, and a small display with a timer. One of my tears falls onto the display.

Noah kneels next to me. "Can you do this?"

"I don't want to die...."

Still holding the Torch, I feel the eyeless screaming and churning around the levels, trying to find a way in to stop me. They're almost all here. All accounted for. Just a few more minutes. I can feel their anger—they're more interested in killing me than going back to their mission.

"It's not so bad," Noah says. "I even think something might come after."

I almost laugh, but it sounds like a choked cry. "You think we have souls?"

He nods. His dark eyes are heavy with tears. "I do." He takes my hand.

Metal screeches below me, followed by the buzz of hundreds of claws on metal.

"They're coming," Noah says.

My finger hovers over the button, trembling. They're all here. I feel it. I just have to push the button. The red button, Gane said. Easy enough. I lay my finger on it gently, then lift it again. Such a simple action. What do I want my final thought to be? What should I look at for the last time? This is my final action. I'm going to press a button, and then I'm going to die. That's it.

Noah's finger presses on top of mine, softly. He's going to do it with me. I look at the button under our fingers.

Just push it, Miranda.

I lower my finger and close my eyes.

The floor explodes under my knees. I fall backward as huge chunks of concrete land around me. The Torch rolls from my grasp. The bomb bounces away, pulling the control pad along by its cord. Beacon is off my back and in my hand. The eyeless climb out of the hole, scrambling over the carpet, shrieking in anger. I kneel as they flow around me like oil. I was too slow; I made a mistake. And now the world will pay for it. I grit my teeth and scream in rage and defiance. It can't end this way. I didn't come all this way to fail.

They stare at me without eyes. They bare their teeth and flex their claws. They come for me. I spring up and snap my arm out, spinning a full circle, feeling resistance as Beacon slices through their hands and faces and necks and bodies. I don't stop. Blood flies around me and eyeless fall. One manages to claw through the armor on my leg. It goes deep in the muscle. I feel the claw click off my femur. I scream so hard something tears in my throat and I taste fresh blood. But I keep spinning. For my friends, who will surely die if I fail. For the world, and the people who will die if I fail. I spin and my sword kills monster after monster, even as they kill me. I burst through the line of eyeless, bleeding from a million different places. My armor is breached and blood flows over the scales freely. My heart pounds, driving it out faster. I'm already dizzy from it, and a little cold. My fingers and toes are numb.

I'm losing blood. The bomb has rolled across the room.

A crippled eyeless swipes my leg from the floor and breaks my shin. It snaps and I go down, fingers tearing at the carpet.

Noah crouches next to me. "C'mon, Miranda. You can do it! You have to do it! Don't give up!"

I pull myself farther along. Noah never leaves my side. "Keep going. Stand up, Miranda. Stand up right now."

The eyeless behind me are a ragged bunch, flopping on the floor in their blood and guts. More are coming up through the hole. My fingers dig at the floor so hard my hands ache. I wiggle up next to the bomb, weak and swimmy, blinking.

I pick up the remote, too dizzy to see straight. Somehow I stand up, all my weight on one leg. I look down and see the hole in my stomach. My blood-slick armor. The pain isn't so bad now. I think that's the blood loss. Can't feel much of anything.

"You can do it," Noah says. He stands next to me, how I remember him. Bright and vibrant and alive. "I believe in you."

He pulls me into a hug and I wrap my arms around him. He isn't really here, but his arms keep me standing all the same. "You can do it," he whispers in my ear. "You're not alone."

The eyeless regroup and surge toward us, circling around like wolves. The nearest one springs, claws outstretched for my throat.

If I push the button, I will save the world.

If I push the button.

I will save the world.

I push the button.

80 COLUMBUS CIRCLE

I lost the girl I loved one month ago, before the cold winds came. Before the snow started to fall, Miranda liked it when my hair was longer, because it curled, so I grew it out, even though she will never see it.

Miranda's sacrifice saved us from annihilation. There is no doubt of that. The world should know her name, but they don't. All they know is fear.

This morning, Noble knocked on my bedroom door. The four of us—Rhys, Sophia, Noble, and me—are living in a fancy New York City apartment. The president, who survived in his bunker, put us here when Noble told him who and what we are. Noble told him it was the most likely location for True Earth to strike next. He promised they'd be back. And they would use eight million people as a meat shield, just like they did in Commander Gane's world.

In my bedroom, Noble said to me: "Peter, I need your assistance. I need you to help me find something. It's important."

"Get Rhys."

I would wait and then fight, but I wasn't interested in seeing anyone, or talking to anyone. I did push-ups and stayed hydrated and stared out my window looking over Central Park. I waited for them to come, with ice in my veins.

He said: "I asked you."

Now I stand amid the wreckage of the Verge. The black sky overhead is endless, a bloated corpse filled with purple worms of lightning. The wind howls between the empty buildings, carrying the scent of rotten meat and dust. The ground is a tumble of boulders and twisted metal. The Verge is a small mountain of broken glass and ash.

No tears come. I save them for the night, when I'm alone. I can picture Miranda's face and hear her voice.

We'll talk, she said to me. *I love you.*

Noble walks through the wreckage, rooting through it with his feet. He has a small data pad in his hand that he references from time to time. I asked him what we were doing out here, but he ignored me. I think about Noah and Miranda and how I didn't get the chance to say good-bye. Some nights

I wake up and forget everything. I sit upright in bed and feel the crush as it all comes back.

I pick up a rock and throw it into what's left of the Verge's moat. The black water eats it whole, then stills.

Noble calls to me a few minutes later. I find my way over the rocks, tired and out of patience. I want to go back to my bed.

He's smiling when I get to him. He leans against a rock taller than himself and laughs.

"Come here."

"What is it?"

"Come here and I'll show you."

He's got something between his thumb and forefinger. I hold out my hand, and he sets it in my palm, gently.

"Careful with that, boy. That's your love."

It's a metal disk the size of a quarter, stamped with an **M**.

ACKNOWLEDGMENTS

Writing sequels is hard, but here are some people who helped make it easier, and whom I am very grateful to know:

Suzie Townsend, Joanna Volpe, Kathleen Ortiz, my high school English teachers (sorry again), Danielle Barthel, Jaida Temperly, Jay Z, Dana Kaye, Catherine Onder, Hayley Wagreich, Laura Kaplan, Dina Sherman, Nellie Kurtzman, Sammy Yuen, Jenn Corcoran, Justin Bieber, Jamie Baker, Pouya Shahbazian, Steve Younger, Kevin Cornish, Tichondrius Horde

Whitney Ross, coffee, Barbara and Travis and Char Char Poelle, Joe Volpe, Susan Dennard, Sarah Maas, Adam "send me your gold" Lastoria, Will "the rectifier" Lyle, Josh Bazell,

Janet Reid, Brooks Sherman, Sean Ferrell, Jeff Somers, the cats Jeff Somers lives with, my loving parents, my brothers and sister